Ghosthunters

and the
Incredibly
Revolting
Ghost!

Ben

Benjamin Borkman

Ghosthunters

and the
Incredibly
Revolting
Ghost!

by CORNELIA FUNKE

Chicken House

SCHOLASTIC INC./NEW YORK

First published in Germany as *Gespensterjäger auf eisiger Spur* by Loewe Verlag
Original text copyright © 1993 by Loewe Verlag
English translation by Helena Ragg-Kirkby copyright © 2006 by Cornelia Funke

Published in the United Kingdom in 2007 by The Chicken House,
2 Palmer Street, Frome, Somerset BA11 1DS.
www.doublecluck.com

Interior illustrations copyright © 2006 by Cornelia Funke

ISBN 0-439-83308-6

12 11 10 9 8 7 6 5 4 3 2   6 7 8 9 10 11/0

Printed in the U.S.A. 40
First Scholastic paperback printing, August 2006
The text type was set in Berthold Baskerville Book.
The display type was set in P22 Kane, Mister Frisky, and Zsazsa Galore.
Interior book design by Leyah Jensen

For
Stefan,
Pascale,
and
Marie

CONTENTS

A Horrible Day

I t all began on one of those days – one of those stupid days when absolutely everything goes wrong.

First thing in the morning, when Tom tried to put on his jeans, he found that his darling sister had knotted the legs. Then he staggered into the bathroom, still half asleep. He brushed his teeth with Mom's face cream and banged his head against a cupboard door that some idiot had left open in the kitchen. Enough disasters to last him an entire day. And he hadn't even had breakfast yet.

Tom often had days like this. Stumbly, bumbly, everything-goes-wrong days. Well, at least everyone else got a good laugh out of them.

"Good morning," said Mom.

"What's so good about it?" snapped Tom.

Lola leaned back, smirking, to watch him. Lola was Tom's big sister – almost six years older than he was, and hopelessly ahead of him in every possible way.

"Hey, watch out, everybody," she said. "Something awful's going to happen to Tom any minute now. It's another of his 'days'!"

Tom gave her a dirty look – and spilled his cocoa down his sweater. Cue shrieks of sisterly laughter.

"Oh Tom," sighed Mom. "Go and get changed."

"Lamebrain!" his sister called after him.

It continued at school, of course. Tom gave everyone a whale of a time. Everyone except himself. On the way home, he stepped in a load of dog-doo, and after he walked into a newsstand, knocking papers all over the pavement, he decided to go straight to bed as soon as he got home. On days like this, bed was the only safe place to be.

But just as he was about to disappear quietly into his bedroom, it happened.

"Tom," said Mom. "Just run down and get some orange juice from the cellar, would you?"

From the cellar.

Mom knew full well that he was scared witless down there. Just the thought of the spiders gave him goose bumps – not to mention what else might be lurking in the darkness.

"Do I have to?" he asked.

"Oh no, don't start with your ghost stories again!" said Mom. "Off you go!"

Merciless. That's what she was. And he wasn't even ten years old yet. Sighing, Tom opened the apartment door.

Tom's family lived in a big building, where every apartment had its own cellar. But Tom was convinced that their cellar was by far the spookiest, the darkest, and the most spider-infested of all. And he knew exactly why.

The caretaker, Mr. Igor Grouchman, hated children. And since Tom and Lola were the only children in the building, their family had been given the most horrendous cellar. Obviously!

Standing outside the dusty door, Tom pursed his lips and boldly adjusted his glasses. The narrow, cold corridor lined by the cellar doors was only dimly lit, and Tom, as always, had trouble getting the wretched key into their lock. The door creaked ominously as Tom pushed it open.

A musty-smelling blackness yawned back at him.

Bravely, he took a step forward and fumbled for the light switch. Where on earth was the blasted thing?

It was an old-fashioned rotary switch, which you could easily sprain your fingers on. *Phew, at last!* There it was. Tom turned it. A pitifully small lightbulb flickered and – *pop!* – exploded into a thousand pieces.

Shocked, Tom stumbled backward – and hit the cellar door with his elbow. *Clunk!* The lock clicked shut. And there he was, standing in the pitch-black cellar, all alone.

Calm! he thought. *Stay calm, Tom. It's just the stupid lightbulb that exploded.*

But since when did lightbulbs just explode?

Tom felt his mouth turn as dry as sandpaper. He tried to take a step backward. But his shoes were stuck to something slimy and wet. He listened to his own breathing, and then heard a quiet rustling. As if something was gently brushing against the old newspapers that Mom had piled up somewhere in the darkness.

"Help!" whispered Tom. "Oh please, help!"

"Aaaaaaahooooo," came a moan from the darkness. Cold, musty-smelling breath chilled his face. And icy fingers gripped his throat.

"Get lost!" cried Tom, lashing out blindly. "Get lost, you disgusting thing!"

The icy fingers let go of his throat and pulled him by his ears. Tom could see something gleaming pale in the darkness. Something with garish green eyes, flapping hair, and a scornful smirk.

A ghost! thought Tom, petrified. *A real ghost!*

"Woooooooooooooooooooooooooh!" howled the dreadful creature.

With desperate strength Tom wrenched his feet free of the glued-down shoes. He staggered to the door

5

and groped with trembling fingers for the bolt. The
gruesome ghoul tugged at his hair and his jacket, and
filled his ears with its terrible howling. With one last
effort Tom pulled the door open; the ghost fell back
with a furious screech – and Tom stumbled out into
the corridor, half dead with shock.

Teased and Scorned!

All at once it was silent.

Dead silent.

Only the door creaked on its hinges. Tom gave it a shove and it slammed shut. He ran to the stairs, his knees shaking. Away! He just had to get away!

Tom had never climbed the three stories faster in his life, though he checked over his shoulder at almost every step. Panting, he reached the apartment and hammered on the door. From above, an indignant Miss Parker peered down at him over the banisters. With her tiny head and pointy nose, she looked like an old crow.

"Well, don't *you* look a mess, Tom," she said disapprovingly.

Tom pushed his glasses straight, ran a hand over his matted hair, and gave her an embarrassed smile.

Then he hammered on the door again.

"Whatever's got into you?" asked Mom, annoyed,

and, to Miss Parker's disappointment, dragged him into the apartment. Exhausted, Tom leaned against the wall.

"I told you!" he blurted out. "I kept telling you, and nobody believed me!" He could only just suppress a sob.

"What did you keep telling me?" asked Mom. "And where are your shoes?"

Lola's bedroom door opened. "Hey, just look at him *this* time," she said, giggling.

"There's a ghost in our cellar!" whispered Tom. "It – it tried to strangle me and . . ."

The rest of his sentence was drowned out by Lola's howling laughter. "A ghost! Wow, Tommy-boy, you really are one of a kind!"

Typical. He had just only narrowly escaped death, and what did he get from his family? Mockery and scorn!

"Leave him alone, Lola!" said Mom, giving Tom that searching look he so hated. "Come on now, what's the matter?"

Tom looked down at his socks. "There's a ghost down there!"

"Lola," said Mom. "Please take Tom back down to the basement and show him that there's absolutely nothing in the cellar except bottles of juice and old newspapers. And get his shoes!"

Horrified, Tom stared at her. "I'm not going back down there! Do you think I'm crazy or what?"

But Mom just opened the door.

Grinning, Lola took his hand and dragged him to the stairs. "Come on," she said. "I want to see your ghost!"

As Tom knew that any further resistance was futile, he followed her.

"It'll kill us," he warned. "You'll see. It'll kill us!"

"Of course!" said Lola.

And then there they were again: in the basement, in front of their cellar door. "Hiya, ghost!" cried Lola, pushing the door open. "Now you're in for it!"

Pitch-black and silent the cellar lay before them. Holding his breath, Tom peeped out from behind Lola's back. But nothing stirred. Absolutely nothing. No "wooooooooooooh"; no icy fingers.

Whistling, Lola took a couple of steps into the darkness. "What's wrong with that wretched light?" she grumbled.

"The lightbulb exploded," whispered Tom. He

was still standing in the corridor while Lola crashed around in the darkness.

"Ugh, what's that stuff?" Tom heard her cursing. "It's all sticky! What were you *doing* down here?"

"Getting two bottles of orange juice," Tom mumbled, taking one cautious step toward the door. But there was no trace of the white something with the garish green eyes and the scornful smirk.

Oh boy, he'd never live this down.

"Here!" said Lola, shoving his shoes at him. The soles were covered with some kind of silvery, shiny, sticky stuff.

"Ghost slime!" whispered Tom.

"Get a life," snorted Lola. "There's probably just some mutant snail in here." Giggling, she vanished into the darkness again. "So where's the orange juice?" she asked.

Tom didn't answer. He was staring at the white hand that had emerged from the darkness and was waving at him.

"There!" he cried. "Look out, Lola!"

Crash! Tom heard the sound of breaking glass in the darkness. "Have you gone raving mad?" screeched Lola, and the next moment she was standing beside him, huffing with rage and holding a broken bottle. "*You* can explain that to Mom. At least three bottles are smashed."

"But there it is again!" cried Tom in desperation. "There, there!" The hand had disappeared.

"You're nuts!" said Lola and slammed the cellar door shut. "You're completely nuts. But I'll tell you one thing: I will not clean up that mess. *You'll* do that. Maybe your *ghost* will help you."

"It's there!" yelled Tom. "I saw it, you stupid cow."

"Yeah, whatever," said Lola, heading for the stairs. "You also saw a flying saucer once, remember, and that turned out to be nothing but an airplane. Ha!"

"But I was only a little kid then!" shouted Tom while he stumbled behind her, shaking with rage.

"You're still a little kid," said Lola, taking the stairs two at a time with her long, slim legs. "And, what's more, you're a lunatic."

Mom cleaned up the mess because of the broken glass. "Otherwise you'll end up cutting yourself on top of everything else!" she said. Then she shook her head and sighed.

Dad said, "That boy has an overactive imagination."

And Lola told everyone that her brother had now officially completely lost it.

But Tom knew what he had seen. He steadfastly refused to go anywhere near the cellar, and just waited for Sunday to arrive. On Sundays Grandma came over for dinner. She listened to him without constantly frowning – unlike his parents.

But he still had three days – and, above all, three nights – to get through until Sunday. During the day Tom barely dared to walk down the stairs; and during the night he just lay in bed with his heart pounding, staring into the darkness. That was the really scary thing about ghosts: You never knew whether they

would simply float through the walls or the ceiling. By Sunday Tom had dark circles under his eyes and was completely exhausted.

"What on earth's the matter with you?" asked Grandma when she saw him. "Are you ill?"

"Of course he isn't – he's just making up stories again," said Lola. "He's been seeing ghosts lately!"

Grandma looked thoughtfully at Tom, took him by the hand, and led him off into his bedroom.

"Well?" she said, folding her short, fat arms. "Fire away, my friend. What happened?"

And Tom told her. About the exploding lightbulb; about the icy fingers and the garish green eyes; about the "wooooooooooooooh" and the white hand that waved at him.

"Hmm!" said Grandma when he had finished. "This is serious business, but I'm afraid I can't help you."

"You can't?" murmured Tom, his head drooping.

"However," said Grandma, tugging at her pearl necklace as she always did when she gave something serious thought, "I do have a friend who knows about ghosts. I'll give you her address."

Perhaps there was some hope left in the world after all.

Hetty Hyssop

The very next Monday, Tom set off after school. He knew that address. It was the same street as the dentist's Mom kept dragging him to. Hopefully that wasn't a bad omen.

Grandma's friend lived in a narrow, dark house with four doorbells. The topmost bell had her name written beside it: HETTY HYSSOP.

I hope she's not as weird as her name, thought Tom as he rang the bell. He had to wait a while for someone to open the door. As he climbed the dark stairs, he had a horribly queasy feeling in his stomach.

Hetty Hyssop was standing in the open door of her apartment, and raised her eyebrows in great astonishment as Tom came puffing up the stairs. She didn't look a bit like Tom's grandma. She was very tall and spindly, with a long, pointy nose and a heap of white curls piled on top of her head.

"A young man!" she said in a deep voice. "Well I never. What brings *you* here?"

"I, uh . . ." Tom made it up the last step and fiddled awkwardly with his glasses, rather embarrassed. "Um, my name's Tom, and my grandma sent me!"

"Aha, your grandma. And who is your grandma, might I ask?"

"Oh right, yeah. Anna Barberry. She said to say hello, and that you might be able to help me. But – um – but I can't pay you very much!"

"Well, you needn't worry about that, young man," said Hetty Hyssop, ushering Tom into her apartment. "It goes without saying that for my best friend's grandson my services are, of course, free."

"I'll just put the kettle on," said the old lady once she had installed Tom in her living room. "Do you take sugar?"

"Yes, please," said Tom. He didn't dare tell her that he didn't drink tea at all.

Whilst Mrs. Hyssop was clattering about in the kitchen, Tom had a quick look around. What a weird apartment! There were mirrors all over the place; even the table had a mirrored top. The sofa and pair of armchairs were such a weird shape that you couldn't quite tell how you were supposed to sit on them. The lamp above Tom's head looked as if it came from another planet. And everything was red. The carpet, the curtains, the wallpaper, the furniture: all red. The only normal thing was a bookshelf.

"Tea is served!" announced Hetty Hyssop, and put a teapot almost as flat as a flying saucer on the mirrored table. The mug she pushed in Tom's direction was crimson. Tom shoveled four spoonfuls of sugar into it, which made the tea taste semi-decent, but the steam misted up his glasses, and after the second sip he was as blind as a mole.

"Well?" asked Hetty Hyssop. "In what matter may I be of assistance, young man?"

Tom hastily cleaned his glasses and shoved them back onto his nose.

"In our cellar—" he saw himself turn bright red in the mirrored tabletop "—in our cellar . . . there's a ghost!"

"Aha!" said his hostess. "May I ask what kind of ghost we're talking about?"

17

"Wh . . . what . . . what kind?" stammered Tom.

"Well now, there are many different types of ghost," said Hetty Hyssop. "What exactly does this one look like?"

Tom looked at her, dumbfounded.

"Well, it was kind of white," he eventually managed. "And it had icy fingers and garish green eyes and – and a hideous grin!"

"How big was it?" asked Hetty Hyssop.

"Pretty big," said Tom. "It almost touched the cellar ceiling!"

"Oh, that's not so very big," Hetty Hyssop replied. "Some ghosts are easily as big as a skyscraper. Did you notice anything sticky on the floor?"

Tom nodded. "My shoes got stuck," he said nervously. That stuff about ghosts as big as skyscrapers was really getting to him.

"Did you get them off the floor again?"

"What?"

"Your shoes!"

"Uh, no. But my sister did."

"Hmm!" Hetty Hyssop tapped her pointy nose. "Just one last question: What exactly did the ghost do?"

"It pulled at me all over," said Tom. Just the

memory of it gave him goose bumps. "And it tried to strangle me with its icy fingers. And made these beastly howling noises."

"Well, no doubt about it, young man," said his hostess, pouring Tom another cup of tea. "There's an ASG in your cellar. An **A**veragely **S**pooky **G**host. That's the good news, you might say. A perfectly routine job for Hetty Hyssop!"

"Does that mean you can get rid of it?" asked Tom. A tidal wave of relief washed over him.

"Oh no, not me!" said the old lady, pulling a fat red book off the shelf. "You're going to get rid of it yourself, young man. With my help!"

That didn't sound quite so reassuring. "So how's that going to happen?" asked Tom.

"Very easily!" said Hetty Hyssop, flicking through the red book and evidently looking for something. "Aha, here it is: 'The Eviction of an ASG.' Pay close attention to this, young man! I'll read it to you. . . ."

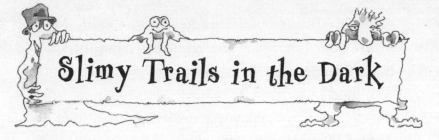

Slimy Trails in the Dark

Tom sat on his bed biting his fingernails.

For the nine hundred ninety-ninth time his gaze wandered to his alarm clock. Ten to eleven.

At eleven sharp he had to be in the cellar. An hour before midnight. That's when ASGs are at their weakest, so Hetty Hyssop had said.

Tom's Ghost Eviction Equipment lay on the carpet in front of him. *Why do I of all people have to get rid of this lousy ghost?* he thought, peeved. *Why didn't it strangle Lola instead?* But complaining wouldn't help, either. The ASG had to go — or he'd never get a wink of sleep again.

Sighing, Tom took off his glasses and cleaned them carefully once more. He'd taken Hetty Hyssop's advice and was wearing only red clothes. That hadn't been easy. He'd "borrowed" the red sweater from his father, and the socks from Lola.

Five to eleven. Tom stuffed the hot water bottle

under his T-shirt. *Yuk!* That felt nasty. Luckily Mom hadn't seen him filling the wretched thing, or she'd have thought there was something seriously wrong with him.

"Heat is an absolutely reliable means to scare off ASGs," Hetty Hyssop had said.

Well, let's hope so, thought Tom. *The thing's a pain in the butt to carry.*

Then he stuck a spare pair of shoes into the back of his belt and hung Mom's circular mirror around his neck. Next he sprayed himself from head to toe in Lola's favorite perfume and tucked Dad's old boom box under his arm.

"Music is a wonderful weapon against the smaller ghosts!" Hetty had said. "But it has to be the right

music. I personally always recommend Mozart – you can't really go wrong with ASGs and Mozart!"

So Tom had purloined some Mozart from his parents. The only thing missing was the raw egg. Carefully Tom slipped it into his sweater pocket.

"Don't take a flashlight, whatever you do, young man!" Hetty Hyssop had warned him. "Flashlights drive ghosts absolutely mad. But you will realize very soon that one can see rather well in the light a ghost exudes."

Tom would have felt a good deal better with a flashlight, but never mind. With one last look around he checked whether he'd forgotten anything. *Boy, I hope nobody sees me like this,* he thought. Then he stuffed a couple of pillows under his blankets to make it look like he was lying in bed, turned off the light, and opened his bedroom door.

It was exactly eleven o'clock.

Nobody spotted him. How could they? Lola was no doubt lying in bed listening to soppy music on her headphones. And Mom and Dad were watching TV.

In the stairwell all was quiet as well. Tom decided not to turn on the lights, just to be on the safe side.

Otherwise he might find Miss Parker peering down at him at any minute. The light from the streetlamps coming in through the corridor window was enough, anyway.

Silently Tom crept past the apartments of Miss Smarmy-Smith, the Pinschermans, and Mr. Rinaldini. He could hear muffled TV noises coming from behind all the doors. *Typical,* thought Tom. *I'm saving the building from a vile ghost, and they're all sitting peacefully in front of their TVs.* Tom released a deep, self-pitying sigh — and then stood stock-still.

There. Just a few steps down, a moldy green shimmery something was dancing in front of Caretaker Grouchman's door.

The Cellar Ghost. No doubt about it.

Tom felt the goose bumps rising despite his hot water bottle. A glistening trail of slime stretched up the dark stairs all the way to Grouchman's doormat, which was so revoltingly slimy that it looked like candy someone had sucked on and spat out again.

I'll just tiptoe back upstairs now, thought Tom. *I'll tiptoe back upstairs as quiet as a mouse. Let stupid old Grouchman sort out that specter! Main thing is, it's gone from our cellar.* But precisely at that moment — when

Tom just wanted to turn around – the ghost looked up at him.

It opened wide its garish green eyes, grew at least six feet high, and stretched its icy fingers out to him.

Tom trembled so much that Dad's sweater slipped off his shoulders. *That's it,* he thought, squeezing his eyes shut. *I'm dead.*

But this time the icy fingers didn't grab him. Instead, a low moaning filled the stairwell. Cautiously Tom opened one eye. The ghost stared into the mirror on his chest, moaned again – and quickly floated back downstairs.

Tom's teeth stopped chattering immediately. The hideous thing was running away! It had run away from him! One–nothing, Tom, and three cheers for Hetty Hyssop! The courage of a lion spread through Tom's wildly beating heart. Certain that victory was his, he rushed past Grouchman's door and down the stairs. The mirror bumped against his chin; the spare shoes jumped out of his belt; the hot water bottle almost slipped out of his sweater; and the whole time he had to avoid those wretched slimy trails. But nothing could stop him. One more flight of stairs and he was in the basement.

Wailing, the ghost rushed down the long, dark corridor – past Igor Grouchman's cellar door, past Miss Parker's, and past Miss Smarmy-Smith's. Then it suddenly turned around, emitted an angry howl, and disappeared – through Tom's cellar door.

Tom braked sharply and gasped for breath. "That," he cried as he unlocked the door with trembling fingers, "will get you nowhere!"

Then he switched on the boom box, turned it up to full volume, and stormed into the cellar accompanied by a pounding orchestra.

"Aaaaaaoooooooooooooooooo!" shrieked the ghost, beating a wobbly retreat into the farthest corner of the room. Tom turned on the freshly installed lightbulb. *Pop!* Once again it exploded into a thousand pieces.

Doesn't matter, thought Tom. *I've almost got it.*

"Aaaaaaaaaarrrgh!" choked the ghost, turning bluish. Probably the effect of Lola's perfume. Tom was groping his way deeper into the dark cellar when the boom box gave up on him. And however desperately Tom shook it he couldn't get a single peep out of it. Bad news. Extremely bad news.

The ghost immediately grew, till it hit the ceiling. "Wooooooooohhhh-hahaha-hahaha!" it howled, puffing

itself up and spitting a revolting yellow liquid onto the
mirror. Then, with a foul smile, it floated over to Tom.

Retreat! thought Tom. *Orderly retreat!* – then he
realized that he was once again glued to the spot. And
his spare shoes were somewhere up on the stairs.
Curses.

"Eeeeeeeeeeeeeeaaaaaaa!" howled the ghost, who
reached for him with his moldy hands – then fell back,
wailing.

The hot water bottle. Two–nothing, Hetty Hyssop.

"Ha – that'll teach you to gloat, you freak!" cried
Tom, whipping the raw egg out of his pocket. "And
I've got something else for you!"

Smash! He hit the ghost right in the center of its pale chest.

"Aaahhhheeee!" it howled, rubbing at the raw egg like mad. And then it began to sob — and shrink. Until it was a whole head smaller than Tom.

"Get out of our cellar!" cried Tom. *"Now!"*

"Noo, noo, noo, nooooo!" sniveled the ghost, pressing its egg-covered fingers over its face. "Have mercy on meeeee, ooohh, please!"

Baffled, Tom set his glasses straight.

"I don't know where else to go!" howled the ghost, hideously rolling its green eyes.

Hetty Hyssop hadn't said anything about sobbing ghosts. Flabbergasted, Tom plonked himself down on a milk crate. Was this some kind of trick? But the ghost really didn't look that dangerous anymore. It even shimmered slightly pinkishly.

"Have you always lived down here?" asked Tom.

"Of course not!" the ghost sniveled irritably, and for a moment its hideous mold color reappeared. "D'you think it's fun living in this third-rate cellar? But —" it started sobbing again "— what choice dooooo I have?"

"What do you mean?" asked Tom. "Where did you live before?"

"None of yooour business!" said the ghost, flickering like a broken lightbulb. "No, absoluuutely none of yooour business!"

"OK, so get lost, then!" said Tom, insulted. "Or I'll go and get a dozen eggs."

"Bully!" sniveled the ghost, rolling its eyes in indignation. "You have a disgusssting personality. My story is far tooooo sad to tell anyone."

"Oh, come on," said Tom. He was starting to feel curious.

"Alright then!" said the ghost, rubbing at the raw egg once more. "But then I can stay here?"

"We'll see," said Tom. "First you have to tell me the story!"

"Disgusssting," the ghost muttered again. But then it sank down onto a pile of old newspapers and began. . . .

A Terrible Story

This is the story Tom learned about on his first ghosthunting night – translated into human language as precisely as possible.

The true home of the ghost who now lived in Tom's cellar was an old villa on the edge of town. The ghost had been haunting the place for more than one hundred fifty years. The big old house was dark and damp; there was a little echo in the entrance hall; and the inhabitants over the years had been wonderfully easy to scare. In short, the ghost had been completely happy there – until a couple of weeks ago. . . .

"It was just before dawn," said the ghost, sniveling. "I was just about to stop scaring folks and go to bed when *it* came! A dreadful ghost. Horrible and mean, oh *sooo* mean! 'I like your house!' it howled, and grabbed me. Then it dragged me onto the roof, took a deep breath, and blew me away. Right out of my own house! My home!" Sobbing, the ghost broke down. But no tears came from its green eyes – just bits of silvery dust.

The ASG could hardly continue its story. The big ghost's breath had sent it whirling right into Tom's street. And since it was already getting light outside, it looked for the darkest, oldest building, and then sneaked into the cellar.

"This one here smelled particularly pleasant – of spiders and woodlice," sniveled the ghost. "But now –" it wrung its pale hands "– now I'm being chased out of here, tooooo. Whatever will become of me?"

Tom took off his glasses and cleaned them. He always did that when he was embarrassed and didn't know what to do next. In fact he felt rather guilty.

"Do you have some kind of name by any chance?" he asked. "Or am I just supposed to call you 'Ghost'?"

"My name is Huuuuuuuuugo," sniffed the ghost.

"Well, that's not a very spooky name!" said Tom, putting his glasses back on.

"So? I can't help my name," Hugo replied. "What's your name, then?"

"Tom!"

"Humph, that's definitely not better!" said Hugo, and started to wail again.

"Stop that! I've got an idea," said Tom. "I know a woman who knows a lot about ghosts. She told me how to, uh –" he felt the blood rushing to his face "– um, that is, she told me what ghosts don't like!"

"Aha! Like raw eggs!" said Hugo, immediately turning his annoyed moldy color.

Embarrassed, Tom set his glasses straight again. "Yeah, yeah, I know. What I'm trying to say is this woman might know how you can chase the big ghost out of your house!"

"You think so?" Hugo began, wobbling around with excitement. "You really think sooooo?"

"I'll ask her first thing tomorrow," said Tom. "And you keep quiet down here, OK? Grouchman's already going to go ballistic when he sees the slime in the stairwell!"

"Paaaaaaah," said Hugo, giving Tom an insulted look, and pushed off behind a sack of potatoes.

Yawning, Tom climbed the cellar steps and opened the door onto the stairwell, no longer expecting dire things to happen. Wrong again.

"Got you, you rascal! So *you're* the culprit!" boomed a familiar voice above his head – and the next moment Tom found himself hanging upside down with his legs waggling around helplessly in the air. "Just you wait, kid!" growled everyone's favorite caretaker, Mr. Igor Grouchman. "Now get scrubbing! For the rest of the night, until your knees ache. And that thing there —" he pulled the boom box out from under his arm "— *that's* disturbing the peace, even if you do sneak off to the cellar to listen to it!"

"Let me go!" snapped Tom, kicking and lashing out all around him. "I haven't done anything!"

"Really?" hissed Grouchman. His hissing sounded even more threatening than his yelling. "Then look at my doormat. And these stairs. Well?" He held Tom,

still kicking, with his nose right above the ghost slime. "How do you explain this mess?"

"That wasn't me!" said Tom, enraged. "Put me down now, or I'll scream!"

"Scream away," said Grouchman, grinning broadly. "Then you can tell your parents what you're doing in the cellar at midnight."

Tom bit his lip. Curses! How was he supposed to explain that one?

"Ha, that shut you up all of a sudden, didn't it?" Grouchman laughed, putting Tom back on his feet. "Now don't you move an inch from there, you hear me? I'm going to get a nice big bucket and rag, and then you can get rid of all that muck, quiet as a mouse and fast as lightning!"

Grinding his teeth and frowning fiercely, Tom nodded. What choice did he have?

He scrubbed the stairwell until three in the morning. While everyone else in the apartment building — his own dear family included — was lying in their warm and surely very comfortable beds.

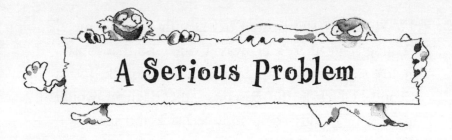

A Serious Problem

"Well, this *is* a surprise!" said Hetty Hyssop as she ushered Tom into her living room for the second time. "Didn't my advice work?"

"Yes, yes. In fact, it worked brilliantly, but . . ." Tom dumped his backpack on the sofa and sat down beside it. "I've got another problem!"

"Aha," said Hetty Hyssop. "Good. I'll make us another pot of tea!" And she'd already disappeared into the kitchen when a white hand snaked through the fabric of Tom's backpack.

"Hey, we had a deal," hissed Tom. "You stay there until I tell you. Got it?"

"It's very uncomfooooortable in here!" said the voice from the backpack.

Hetty Hyssop stuck her long nose around the door. "By the way, young man," she said, "you can tell that ghost in your backpack to come out!"

Tom looked at her, speechless.

Hetty Hyssop twisted her mouth in amusement. "Young man, there's no way I can miss that musty, moldy smell even if it's hiding in a backpack. Just a second: I'll close the curtains – the daylight would make your ghostly companion feel sick and sneezy on the spot."

Of course the curtains were red, like everything else in the strange room.

Hugo floated out of his hiding place with an embarrassed grin, looked around – and crumpled up, horrified.

"Aaaargh, ooohooooooo, aaaaargh!" he howled,

pressing his white hands in front of his face. "What a dreadful room! Nothing but horrible red and mirrors everywhere. Dreadful!"

"I'm sorry," said Hetty Hyssop, "but I quite often have to deal with seriously dangerous ghosts. And they tend to find this room pretty off-putting!"

"Oohoooo, I can't stand it!" wailed Hugo. And — *whoosh* — he disappeared back into Tom's backpack. Hetty Hyssop shrugged and went to fetch the tea from the kitchen.

"Let's talk about your second problem, young man," she said as once more Tom shoveled revolting amounts of sugar into his tea. "I presume it has to do with your companion there."

"Too right!" said Tom, and told her the whole sad tale.

When he had finished, Hetty Hyssop wore quite a serious expression on her face and was fiercely kneading her pointy nose. "Well, well, well," she said. "I think I know which house we are talking about. Not long ago, I passed an old villa that smelled exceptionally strongly of ghosts. I'm afraid you have really got a problem on your hands this time."

Tom's heart missed a beat. "What – what do you mean?"

"Well, this extremely repulsive ghost who chased your companion away is clearly an IRG, or Incredibly Revolting Ghost, as the full technical term for this species goes. And goodness knows, young man, you don't mess around with an IRG!"

Tom swallowed. "That means we . . . can't do anything? Hugo has to stay in our cellar?"

Quiet sobbing came from inside the backpack.

"Oh no, that's not what I said," replied Hetty Hyssop. "I only pointed out that picking a quarrel with an IRG is very dangerous. Extremely dangerous – even for a professional ghosthunter. With this species you won't get very far using mirrors, music, and raw eggs!"

"So," Tom hardly dared to ask, "what works against IRGs?"

Hetty Hyssop kneaded her nose until it was as red as her living room. "Well, there's only one thing I know of," she said. "Graveyard dirt!"

Tom looked at her, dumbfounded. "Come again?"

"Graveyard dirt. At least a bucketful. Yes – and

you'll also have to practice squinting, young man. Squinting can save your life if you meet an IRG."

The old lady stood up and went over to her bookshelf. "I'll give you something to take with you," she said, pulling out a small book. "You'll find in here a very instructive list of the known characteristics, likes, and dislikes of ASGs and IRGs. Chapter Two, if I remember rightly. Study it carefully!"

She handed him the book, but Tom shook his head. "No," he said hoarsely. "No, thanks. Let's forget the whole thing. As far as I'm concerned, Hugo can stay in our cellar until the end of time. I think I'd rather go home now!"

The sobbing in Tom's backpack turned into a wailing and gnashing of teeth.

"That's a pity, young man," said Hetty Hyssop. "I just wanted to offer you my help!"

Tom looked at her, confused. "But you said it was terribly dangerous!"

"Oh well!" The old woman shrugged. "Life is dangerous, isn't it? And I feel a bit sorry for your pale friend here. If we're well enough prepared, we'll have no trouble banishing this IRG!"

"And what about the graveyard dirt?" asked Tom. This was what was getting to him most at the moment.

"Oh, that's no problem. We can get it tonight."

"Tonight?" Tom frowned. "Why during the night?"

"Oh, did I forget to mention that? Only dirt gathered at night works against IRGs. What do you think? Shall we meet tonight outside the gate to the graveyard at around eleven?"

"I . . . um . . . I don't know!" stammered Tom.

"You could get your Cellar Ghost to fly you there." Hetty Hyssop looked down the end of her long nose, examining Tom.

"I'm not a Cellar Ghost!" came an offended voice from inside the backpack. "But I'd be deeeelighted to help!"

"What do you mean, 'fly'?" asked Tom faintly. His head was starting to spin.

"Ghosts normally fly, don't they!" came the muffled voice from the backpack. "Or do you think I float on fooooot?"

"So what do you think, young man?" Hetty Hyssop stretched her long, thin hand out to Tom.

"Shall we teach this IRG some manners together so that your ghostly friend can go back home?"

What was Tom supposed to say? "OK," he mumbled, grasping Hetty Hyssop's hand.

A sigh of relief escaped from the backpack.

The Book of Ghosts

"**S**ince when do you cart around your backpack with you for the whole afternoon?" asked Lola when Tom got home.

"Mind your own business," he growled.

"Oh, but it *is* my business!" said Lola. *Snatch!* Before he could stop her, she'd torn the backpack out of his hand and was peering curiously inside. "Nothing, nothing at all," she said, disappointed.

"Of course there's nothing. I used to keep my ghost in there," said Tom, "and it's been back in the cellar for ages now."

"Hilarious. Totally hilarious!" retorted Lola, annoyed, and plonked herself down in front of the TV.

Relieved, Tom went to his room and shut the door. Then he pulled Hetty Hyssop's book out from under his sweater, flung himself down on the bed, and started, as advised, to read Chapter Two. This is what he found:

CHARACTERISTICS OF ASGs AND IRGs

This chapter deals with two very interesting and distantly related types of ghosts: the Averagely Spooky Ghost (abbreviated to ASG) and the Incredibly Revolting Ghost (abbreviated to IRG). ASGs are seen quite frequently, whereas IRGs are extremely rare – which is just as well, because IRGs are also extremely difficult to get rid of, in addition to being highly dangerous. An ASG can be expelled – under expert advice – by a beginner. However, beginners are strongly urged NOT to attempt expelling an IRG. Such an undertaking is LETHALLY DANGEROUS. Only highly qualified ghosthunters, equipped with nerves of steel and a vast body of knowledge, can approach an IRG and – given the right conditions – successfully expel it. Listed below are the abilities, likes, and weaknesses of both ASGs and IRGs, which will hopefully demonstrate this case, and may also persuade the honorable reader of the need for the utmost caution.

ASG	IRG
Passes through walls up to two feet thick	Passes through walls of any thickness
Is afraid of mirrors	Avoids mirrors: Hiding behind them may save a ghosthunter's life
Flies about as fast as a crow	Pursues its victim with the speed of a jet plane

ASG	IRG
Appearance causes goose bumps and teeth-chattering	See ASG; plus, its appearance causes the hair to stand on end, all over-body trembling, and a constant desire to look over one's shoulder
Icy fingers provoke mild trembling	Freezes humans solid with its icy breath
Moves objects of up to 100 pounds with one look	Moves any heavy object with one look, and sends it flying through the air
Makes goose-bump-provoking noises	Makes teeth-shattering, heartbeat-stopping noises
Can inflate itself up to ten feet high	Can inflate itself to the size of a skyscraper
Makes small machines (telephones, kitchen gadgets, irons) go haywire	Likes turning off radios and TVs, and makes large machines (building site vehicles, cranes, railways, carousels) go haywire

ASG	IRG
Emits unpleasant musty smells	Emits a terrible stink that causes a rash (blue spots)
Likes smashing lightbulbs, flower vases, and coffee tables	Likes smashing lightbulbs, plus any large objects: So take special care! Never look an IRG in its yellow eyes: it might make you explode!
Gives off snail-like sticky slime	Leaves a glittery trail behind that sticks better than the best superglue
Doesn't like warmth; flees from hot water bottles, hot tea, and radiators	Also dislikes warmth, but doesn't flee; instead, it becomes wild with anger and goes doubly berserk
Panics when confronted by raw eggs	Just laughs at raw eggs
Feels sick and sneezy in daylight	Daylight does IRGs no harm

Detests perfume smells; reacts to them with nausea and by changing color and retreating	Spraying it directly with violet perfume mostly causes the IRG to retreat or temporarily disappear
Fears and avoids graveyards; turns to dust on contact with dirt from said graveyards	Graveyard dirt is supposed to be the most effective means of driving out an IRG; however, nothing more definite than that is known

As said before, we hope that this list has convinced the honorable reader once and for all that an encounter with an IRG is to be avoided at all costs. If, however, a ghosthunter should still be so daring as to ignore this book's explicit advice and pick a fight with one of these grisly creatures, all we can do is hope that he has more luck than judgment.

That was all. Tom snapped the book shut with a frown. He rolled over onto his back and stared at the ceiling.

Had he gone nuts? Why on earth was he letting himself get involved in such a hair-raising adventure? Just because of a ghost that had scared the life out of him and almost strangled him with its icy fingers? Thanks to which his entire family now believed him to be a lunatic? The ghost whose disgusting slime he had spent half a night scrubbing off the stairwell?

No.

Tom sat up decisively.

Out of the question. No way. Let that old disgusting spook stay down in the cellar. He wasn't afraid of him anymore. Only someone with a death wish would take on an IRG, that was for sure, no matter what Hetty Hyssop said. He'd better tell Hugo right away. Then the whole ghastly episode would be behind him once and for all.

"Where are you off to now?" asked Lola as Tom sneaked out of the apartment once more.

"To play with my ghost," he replied, and slammed the door behind him.

A Wailing and Gnashing of Teeth

"Hey!" whispered Tom, feeling his way into the dark cellar. "Hey, Hugo, where are you?"

"What do yoooou want?" came a sleepy voice from the darkest corner.

"I, um . . ." Tom cleared his throat, embarrassed. "I have to talk to you."

"Can't it wait?" grumbled the ghost. Flickering, he rose from behind the potato sack. When he yawned, Tom saw nothing but the cellar wall through his open mouth.

"Oh, you can go back to sleep in a minute," said Tom. "I just wanted to tell you –" he bit his lip "– that I'm not coming tonight!"

Hugo looked at him, gobsmacked. "Do yoooou mean yoooou're not going to help me anymore?"

"I'm sorry," said Tom. "But you can stay here for now. Good night!"

Quickly he made for the door. He wished he could have just sunk into the cellar floor with shame.

"Aaaaaaaaaooooooooooooeeeee!" howled Hugo behind him. "Aaaaooo, betrayed and abandoned! It's disgraceful! Booooo hooooo!"

"Shh! Keep it down!" hissed Tom.

"Oooooooooh!" yowled the ghost, wobbling around and wringing his hands. "Ooooooh, yoou're afraid, yoou're just afraid!"

The whole cellar was filled with his flickering blue ghostly light.

"Yeah, that's right," said Tom. "Dead right. So? You're afraid, too. I'm not even ten yet, and there's no way I'm going to get frozen solid or blown up. No thanks!"

"Ooooooooohhhhhh!" moaned Hugo. Such floods of silvery dust streamed from his eyes that Tom had to sneeze. "Yoou're so mean, yoou're so incredibly mean."

"No I'm not!" Tom said defensively. "What's more, I don't know what you're making such a fuss about. You've still got Hetty Hyssop. She'll be better at helping you than I will, anyway."

"She won't help me now, either," wailed Hugo. "Huuumans always stick together, don't think I don't know that! I'll have to spend the rest of my life in this stinking cellar, booo hoooo!"

"It didn't stink until you lived here," growled Tom, setting his glasses straight. How annoying – he really felt sorry for Hugo.

"Oh! Oooooooh! Oooooow!" sniffed the ghost, tearing at its shaggy hair. The noise really was almost unbearable.

"Come on, give it a rest," said Tom uneasily. "It's not that bad down here."

"Oh no?" A voice suddenly came from behind him. Shocked, Tom whirled around – and saw Lola's grinning face.

"Well, I wouldn't much enjoy sitting around in the dark." Curiously she looked past Tom, but the cellar was empty. Hugo had vanished without a trace. And this time Tom was glad.

"I'm seriously worried about you, little brother," said Lola mockingly. "What do you think Mom'll say when she hears you're sitting in the cellar talking to yourself, huh?"

"I'm not talking to myself," Tom replied casually. "I'm talking to the ghost. It's pretty lonely down here, after all."

"Oh!" Irritated, Lola folded her arms across her chest. "So what do you two talk about?"

"Oh, we'd actually just finished our conversation, hadn't we, Hugo?" he said to the potato sack. "Take care, buddy. And forget what I said. That IRG will soon meet its masters and you will go home."

The cellar was deadly silent.

"Come on!" Tom shoved Lola back out into the corridor. "I want some sleep now."

"Oh jeepers," moaned Lola, shaking her head. "It's a thousand times worse than I thought!"

A Bucketful of Graveyard Dirt

Yet another night with no sleep, thought Tom as he put on his jacket. *I don't think I'll ever be able to close my mouth again for yawning.*

Once again, nobody noticed him slipping out of the apartment. But this time, Hugo came floating up to him right outside Miss Smarmy-Smith's door.

"Why didn't you wait in the cellar?" hissed Tom.

"Why should I? Do yooooou want to fly underground?" asked the ghost, puffing his musty breath into Tom's face. "The best place to take off will be over there!" And, quietly humming to himself, he floated over to one of the hall windows.

"Out of there?" asked Tom – and stepped in the wretched ghost slime again. "Curses!" he muttered, tugging at his shoe. "Why do you always have to leave this mess behind?"

Hugo looked at him, offended. "Don't be such a smart aleck! Yoooou'd better open that window for us."

"Yeah, yeah." Tom obeyed, and looked down onto the dark street. "That's quite a drop!"

"Oooh, quite a drop. Oooooooh!" said Hugo teasingly, and floated out into the night.

"I don't get how this is supposed to work," whispered Tom. "Do I sit on your back or what?"

"Of cooourse not!" Hugo purred. "Yooou climb onto the windowsill, I put my arm around yooou, and – *wheeeeee!* We're off! Easy as pie!"

"For you, maybe!" growled Tom, climbing onto the windowsill. *Don't look down*, he told himself. *Just don't look down*. But Hugo had already slung his icy arm around him and floated out into the cool September night, pressing Tom like a sack of potatoes against his

pale chest. Beneath them trees and houses shrank to the size of toys. Quite a disturbing sight.

"Hey, why are you flying so high?" cried Tom. But Hugo just laughed a hideous laugh and floated on. Thank goodness their spooky flight didn't take too long.

The graveyard lay at the northern edge of town. With a howl Hugo flew over the iron gate and set Tom down in the small square behind it. One solitary lamp spread its dim light into the night, illuminating some of the gravestones. Tom had only one wish: to be back in his bed, to know nothing about ghosts and ghosthunting. Strangely even Hugo seemed a little nervous, probably because of what Tom had read about ASGs in *The Book of Ghosts*: "turns to dust on contact with dirt from graveyards."

Not a pleasant prospect, even for a ghost.

Tom shivered, trying to make himself believe it was just the cool night air. He had often been here with his grandma, visiting his grandpa's grave, but that was always during the daytime, of course. At night this was quite a different place.

"Good evening, young man," said a voice, and Hetty Hyssop emerged from the darkness carrying an old-fashioned lantern and a bucket.

Baffled, Tom glanced at the enormous chain around the graveyard gate. "How did you get in?"

"Oh, I have my secret ways." The old lady smiled meaningfully. "After all, I come here quite often. But don't let's stand around talking. It's very cold tonight!"

"I'll wait here!" said Hugo. "I don't like graveyards. Not in the slightest."

"Well, that's because you are not a Graveyard Ghost," Hetty Hyssop observed. "Just don't put your moldy feet onto one of the graves or we may have to carry you home in a bucket, too! Come on, Tom!" She thrust the bucket into Tom's hands while Hugo seated himself on the gate with a horrified expression, then made for one of the narrow paths that wound through the maze of graves.

"Hey – the bucket's full!" said Tom, astonished, while he tried to keep up with the old woman's long, spindly legs.

"Of course it is!" she answered, glancing around. "I always bring replacement dirt with me. Oh, here we go. I do believe this is a good spot!" With a confident smile she sped over to a grave that lay slightly off the path and looked extremely overgrown. "I only take dirt from forgotten graves like this one," she explained while she poured out the dirt she had brought and plucked the grass up from the old grave. Then she filled the bucket with new graveyard dirt and pulled a small flowerpot out of her big handbag. "We'll leave this here as a little thank-you! Ghosthunters should always be respectful of the dead. Remember that, Tom, even if from time to time you have to hunt them down."

Whilst Hetty Hyssop quietly planted her flower, Tom looked around nervously. There was a huge gravestone on the next grave and in front of it stood a colored grave light with a small door to push a candle inside. The little door suddenly opened – and something floated out. Something sulfurous yellow with red eyes. Barely bigger than Tom's hand.

"Hetty Hyssop!" he whispered, his eyes fixed on the creature.

"What's the matter, young man?" the old lady asked while she grabbed for a tissue to rub the dirt off her fingers.

"Some . . . some . . . thing came out of that grave light!" Tom stuttered. "Something yellow with – with eyes. It's floating right at us!"

"Oh that!" Hetty Hyssop seemed utterly unim-

pressed. "Don't take any notice of it. That's just a Graveyard Ghost. Totally harmless, but very curious. The poor things spend most of their ghostly existence horrendously bored. Come on! Let's go back to your friend."

And off they set with their full bucket. Tom kept stumbling over his own feet because he couldn't stop looking at the Graveyard Ghosts. There were more and more of them. As soon as Tom passed one of the grave lights, its inhabitant came out and fluttered after them. Some were blue, others purple, or as yellow as the first one, obviously depending on the color of their homes. There was a whole flock of them and they giggled – at least that's how Tom interpreted the shrieky little noises they made from time to time.

The tiny specters accompanied the two ghost-hunters until they reached the little square behind the entrance again, but there they suddenly disappeared, as if they had turned into thin air.

"Please, those pathetic Graveyard Ghosts!" Hugo mocked, floating down from the gate. "Who're they trying to scare?"

"Well, I know this thought is not easy to grasp for

an ASG," Hetty Hyssop said, "but not all ghosts' lives revolve around scaring people."

"Oh yes?" Hugo answered – and backed away, horrified, when she set down the full bucket of dirt. "Aaaaaaaaaaargh!" he howled. "What are you trying to do? Turn a poor ghost to dust?"

"Oh, don't make such a fuss," Hetty replied. "I'll take the dirt home with me. All you've got to do is make sure our friend here gets safely back to his bed." Then she turned to Tom. "Young man, we've taken the first step on our hunt. Tomorrow evening we'll take the next one, which will be far more dangerous. We'll meet at seven at your ghostly friend's former home to confront the IRG and, if possible, eliminate it before it haunts another place. Wear something warm, and practice squinting! I'll take care of the rest. Agreed?"

Tom nodded. But Hugo was off again, grumbling and groaning. "Not until tomorrow?" he howled. "Why not now? Am I supposed to spend another night in that stinking cellar? With nothing but a couple of mice to scare?"

"My dear ghostly friend," said Hetty Hyssop tartly,

"if you keep moaning like that, I feel quite tempted not to help you at all. Good night, Tom!" And with that she turned and tramped off into the darkness without another word.

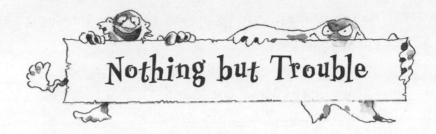

Nothing but Trouble

Next morning, Tom fell asleep in his English class. He was sitting in the back row, so he might have gotten away with it. But unfortunately he also snored very loudly. Quite embarrassing. His English teacher just shook him awake, but in Math another noisy nap landed Tom extra homework.

So that was what you got for rendering heroic services to a homeless ghost! Never mind that it also proved ghosthunting and going to school were hardly compatible.

At dinner Tom was yawning so much that he could barely eat his macaroni, which earned him a very suspicious look from his mother. "You've been reading under the covers again, Tom!"

Tom shook his head vigorously – and yawned.

"Well, something must have made you this tired," said Dad.

"He's probably been playing with his ghost," Lola said with a smirk.

"Oh Tom, you don't still believe there's a ghost in the cellar?" asked Mom, concerned. "Is that why you can't sleep at night?"

"Of course not!" said Tom, frowning at his sister. "I'm just –" he had to yawn again "– dead tired. You are tired all the time, too, aren't you?" And with that he headed off to his room.

Slimy situation, thought Tom. *I need an alibi for this evening. Who knows how long it'll take to drive out an IRG. And as things stand, Mom'll definitely come to check whether I'm asleep. Curses!* He took the tiny makeup mirror that he had nicked from Lola out of his pocket and practiced squinting. But that didn't make thinking of an alibi any easier. Just when he was feeling quite queasy from staring at his nose, his darling sister came crashing into his room. Without knocking, naturally.

"Hey, stop squinting at me," she snapped. "Grandma's on the phone – she wants to talk to her little lunatic of a grandson!"

Tom pushed past her, still squinting. Grandma. That could be the solution to his alibi problem! Luckily

Mom collared Lola to clean up in the kitchen, so he could talk to Grandma in peace and quiet.

Of course she had called to hear all about his ghost. Tom gave her a full report before bringing up his new problem. But Grandma, sadly, wasn't eager to give him an alibi for the night.

"No," she said. "That sounds dangerous, my boy. I don't want to be a part of it."

"Please, Grandma. You don't have to lie. I *will* sleep at your house, honest. I'll just get there a bit later."

"No!"

"Please?"

"No. Unless –" Grandma cleared her throat "– unless Hetty tells me that it's not too dangerous. I'll ask her, then I'll call you back!"

A couple of minutes later, Grandma rang again. "Hetty says it's OK!" she said. "In fact she seems quite impressed by your ghosthunting skills. Hand me over to your mother!"

Tom had secured his alibi.

Homework took forever, thanks to the wretched extra Math assignment. It was already half past six when

Tom slipped into the sitting room to snatch the street map from the chest of drawers. Luckily Hugo had remembered the address of his beloved villa, 23 Nightshade Walk. It was even farther away than Tom had thought. Beyond the city's central park. Curses! He'd be late. Tom quickly shoved the street map under his sweater, jumped up – and ran straight into Lola's folded arms.

"Well, squirt," she said, "what's the street map for?"

"Mind your own business!" Tom angrily shoved her aside and ran back into his room. How did she always manage to sneak up on him so quietly? He grabbed his backpack and the bag he'd stuffed his winter clothes into. His fingers trembled with anger as he put on his shoes. Big sisters should be banned! As Tom was about to go, Lola appeared again, leaning against the living room door, grinning. "So, you're taking your backpack with you again? And what's in that other bag?"

Tom just ignored her and shut the apartment door in her face. At least she didn't follow him to the cellar.

It was already ten to seven when Tom left the house with Hugo in his backpack. With hasty steps he made his way out of the narrow inner city with all its nooks and crannies, through the park, and then through streets that he knew only from a couple of Sunday walks. He put on his jacket at a bus stop and knotted his scarf, but the gloves he left in his pockets. He'd be conspicuous enough as it was.

The hedges became longer and higher and the houses fewer and fewer, but no Nightshade Walk turned up. Tom looked at the street map and cursed under his breath. Sweat dripped from his forehead. Winter clothes, boom boxes, violet perfume . . . ghost-hunting was definitely a weird business.

"Oh blast!" he muttered. "I probably should've turned right ten blocks ago." Nervously he looked around, trying to find a street sign – and saw Lola. She quickly hid herself behind a bush, but she was not fast enough.

"Come out!" Tom bellowed across the road. "Come out — I saw you!"

Casually she stepped out, a broad, big-sister grin on her face.

"Keep your shirt on, shorty," she said mockingly. "I'm just going for a nice little walk. And what about you? Are you off to the North Pole?"

What was he supposed to do? Tom looked desperately at his watch. Ten past seven! He was late. Oh blast! If only he could set Hugo on her! But the ghost was no use at all in the daylight.

"Hello? Have you grown roots?" cried Lola.

Tom took off his glasses, cleaned them, and cursed once again to himself. And then he had an idea. A brilliant idea.

"I just noticed I went the wrong way," he said, looking at the street map as cluelessly as possible. "You know this part of town quite well, don't you?"

"Yeah, of course I do," said Lola. "A couple of kids in my class live here!"

Bingo! She'd taken the bait.

"Doesn't that guy with the spaghetti hair live

around here?" Tom asked innocently. "Yes, I remember. He lives on a street with a really funny name. Ted . . . Toad . . ."

Lola went as red as a rose hip.

"Tadpole Terrace! Yes, that's it!" cried Tom, waving around his street map. "You told us that at dinner once. That's right here, around the corner!"

"So?"

Tom closed the map. "Well, let's put it this way: If you keep spying on me, I'll go and visit Spaghetti Hair to tell him that my poor big sister has a big crush on him!"

For a moment, Lola was speechless. Had this ever happened before? Tom couldn't remember. She went as chalk-white as Hugo's pale hands, then red again, like a freshly plucked poppy, then back to white. Tom savored every single second.

"You wouldn't dare!" Lola said furiously.

Tom shrugged. "Wanna bet?"

Lola chewed her lip angrily. "I couldn't care less where you're going, anyway, you stupid baby!" she hissed. Then she turned and stormed off.

The Haunted Villa

When Tom arrived at 23 Nightshade Walk, he was completely out of breath and Hetty Hyssop was looking quite annoyed. She was standing in front of the wrought-iron gates wearing a thick winter coat with gloves and scarf. The bucket of graveyard dirt stood beside her and over her shoulder she carried a heavy bag stuffed with whatever a professional ghost-hunter carries around. Tom gave it a curious glance.

"A bit more punctuality wouldn't go amiss, young man," she said. "It's already twenty past seven and in the ghosthunting business the right moment quite often may be the difference between life and death. Luckily you arrived before dark!"

"I – I got lost!" panted Tom, quickly putting on his gloves. "And then I had to shake off my sister!"

"Very well, let's forget it!" said Hetty. "In any event, we've got the right address. I've never smelled

such a strong IRG vapor in my whole ghosthunting career!"

This definitely didn't make Tom's heart beat any slower. Disconcerted, he peeped through the heavy wrought-iron gates. The old villa that had once been Hugo's home stood amongst high, dark trees, and looked anything but inviting. Its narrow, dark windows stared at Tom like dead eyes, and only the white smoke billowing out of the chimneys gave away the fact that someone was living there. Why, though, would anyone light a fire on this warm, late summer night?

"Come on, young man! Let's have a closer look," said Hetty Hyssop, grabbing the bucket. The heavy gates squeaked as they swung open. "Oh, what a lovely sound!" moaned Hugo, in raptures, from Tom's backpack. "I'm back home again. Oooooooh, I think I'm going to cry."

"Don't you want to get out?" asked Tom as they approached the house. The nearer they got, the more forbidding it looked.

"Too light, it's much too light," grumbled Hugo.

"Well, I wouldn't exactly describe it as 'light,'" said Tom. The gigantic trees cast dark shadows and it was cold under their massive branches. Tom shivered and looked once again at the dark windows. What if the IRG was already watching them?

A set of wide, moss-covered steps led up to the front door. Hetty Hyssop put down her bucket and pressed the ornate doorbell decisively. The stained brass plate above it read: ZACHARY LOVELY.

Nothing stirred.

Which made Hetty frown. "Hugo, you said Mr. Lovely worked from home, didn't you?"

"And it's true!" said the backpack. "He only ever works from home!"

"Hmm, very fishy!" Hetty Hyssop pressed her nose against the window next to the front door.

"Can you see anything?" Tom fiddled nervously with his glasses.

"Just the usual traces of IRGs!" Hetty quietly replied. "Overturned furniture, carpets covered in slime. But no sign of Mr. Lovely!"

"Ooooohoooo!" Hugo wailed. "That dreadful ghost has probably frozen him or blown him to pieces!"

"Nonsense!" said Hetty Hyssop. "Even an IRG needs someone to scare. I suspect Mr. Lovely has hidden somewhere." She took a flat tin out of her bag.

"Here you go, young man. Smear this on the soles of your shoes. First-rate anti-IRG-slime cream. And this —" she said, holding out a small clear cube to Tom "— put it in your jacket pocket. It's an IRG sensor. As soon as you get near to one, it'll turn as cold as ice. I've got one, too. Very useful."

The cube felt pleasantly warm. Tom quickly stowed it away.

"And what about me?" asked Hugo, offended. "I need a sensor like that, tooooo!"

"Nonsense!" growled Hetty Hyssop while she bent down to examine the door lock. "You're a ghost. You'll know when your colleague gets close to us." She rummaged around in her pocket and pulled out a small piece of wire.

"This'll have to do," she muttered, and carefully pushed the wire into the lock.

"Do you, um, do you often pick locks?" asked Tom, wondering whether this was a typical ghosthunter skill, too.

"Of course! My clients are mostly so rigid with fear that they can't even manage to open their doors."

Click! The heavy door sprang open.

"Come on, Tom," Hetty whispered. "This is where things get serious."

An icy cold met them when they stepped into the house. Icy cold and a deathly silence. They had entered a high, gloomy hall with only two small windows to let the daylight in. The ghost slime on the carpets shimmered in the dim light like a tangle of giant snail trails. The sweeping staircase up to the first floor was completely covered with the gooey stuff. In the middle of the hall a big table lay like a beetle on its back, stretching its legs in the air. A cupboard was standing on its head. All the pictures on the walls hung askew. And high above them, the chandelier swung slowly to and fro. To and fro.

Tom's fingers curled tightly around the cube. It was still warm. Reassuringly warm.

There were five doors: two on the left, two on the right, and one at the very farthest end of the eerie hall.

"Come out, Hugo!" Hetty Hyssop whispered into Tom's backpack. "Where does Mr. Lovely mostly spend his time?"

Wobbling, his face pale yellow, Hugo appeared.

"In the drawing room oooooor in the kitchen," he breathed. "Second door on the left, then there's a dooooor behind it. Oooooohooooo, this place is in a terrible state!"

Quietly Hetty Hyssop put her fingers to her lips before she silently opened the drawing room door and peeped inside. Then she gestured to Tom and Hugo to follow her.

It was warm in Mr. Lovely's drawing room, pleasantly warm, as a big fire was burning in the fireplace. Mellow evening sunlight poured through two windows.

"Uooooooogh!" howled Hugo, and disappeared back into the backpack on the spot.

"Mr. Lovely?" asked Hetty Hyssop quietly. "Are you there? We've come to help you."

Tom thought he heard a sniffle, and then a man

with tangled gray hair suddenly peeped out from behind the sofa. "Who — who are you?" he asked.

"My name is Hetty Hyssop," the old lady introduced herself. "I'm a professional ghosthunter."

"Oh really? But that's . . ." Mr. Lovely struggled to his feet and looked incredulously at the old woman. He was tall and fat and wore a black suit covered all over with flour. "How do you know about my misfortune?" Anxiously he looked over his shoulder. "It's all quiet at the moment. But that's deceptive. You've just come at a good moment."

"I know, I know." Hetty Hyssop smiled. "It's all a question of planning. There's just one time of day when IRGs aren't particularly active — between seven and eight in the evening."

"You don't need to tell me that!" groaned the befloured Mr. Lovely. "It's the only time I get any work done. It's a catastrophe!" He ran his trembling fingers through his hair. "You see, I'm a cookie inventor, and my newest cookie recipe, 'Fairy Kisses,' is — oh dear me! My cookies!" Horrified, he slapped himself on the forehead, rushed to the door, peeped out — and disappeared into the hall.

"Well, *he's* a bit of a weirdo," said Tom.

"Clear symptoms of an IRG attack," said Hetty Hyssop. "Come on, let's draw the curtains, then maybe our Cellar Ghost will dare to come out again. We should introduce him to Mr. Lovely."

"I'm not a Cellar Ghost. How many times do I have to tell yooooou that?" came an annoyed voice from inside the backpack.

Mr. Lovely's curtains were thick and blue. Once they were shut, the fire in the hearth sent flickering shadows around the dark room.

"Home sweet home!" sighed Hugo, and floated up to the ceiling with an enraptured expression.

Just at that moment Mr. Lovely came rushing back into the drawing room. "I'm sorry!" he cried breathlessly. "But I absolutely had to go and see to my 'Fairy Kiss' cookies. Why've you made it so dark?"

"Woooooooooooooohhh!" With a triumphant howl Hugo wobbled toward Mr. Lovely clad in his most disgusting moldy colors.

"Oh no, please, not again!" cried Mr. Lovely, covering his face with his hands. "No, I can't stand it!"

"Hugo!" cried Tom angrily.

"But I just wanted to scare him a little bit," Hugo protested. "Just like in the old days."

Mr. Lovely slumped, trembling, onto his flour-covered sofa. "Oh," he sobbed. "What have I done to deserve this?"

"Calm down, my dear!" said Hetty Hyssop. "We've come to help you. And I promise that this Cellar Ghost —" she gave Hugo a withering 'this house is already haunted' look "— won't scare you like that again!"

"I'm not a Cellar Ghost!" muttered Hugo, but he floated remorsefully back into Tom's backpack.

"I just don't get it," moaned Mr. Lovely. "I've not understood anything for a long while now. And my cookies —" a fat tear rolled down his cheek "— my cookies don't taste very nice anymore, either. How's a serious cookie-maker supposed to work under such conditions? I've not invented a single kind since, since . . ." He started sobbing again.

". . . since this house has been haunted in a very serious way," Hetty Hyssop finished his sentence.

"Yes! Yes, indeed!" Mr. Lovely nodded. "Even my grandfather reckoned that there were strange goings-on in this house. He suspected my late great-great-uncle Hugo of haunting the place after he fell off the roof while sleepwalking. A little family ghost, so to speak. But for the last week it's been unbearable!" Mr. Lovely shook his head in desperation. "I'm in such a state that I put salt into the dough instead of sugar, capers instead of chocolate, laundry detergent instead of flour. I even burned the cookies four times!" Mr. Lovely covered his face once again with his floury hands. "Before long no cookie factory in the world will buy my recipes!"

Hetty Hyssop nodded sympathetically. "My dear Mr. Lovely," she said, "the spook manifestations you faced last week had nothing to do with your uncle Hugo. I'm sorry to tell you that you've been the victim of an IRG invasion."

Mr. Lovely raised his head. "Pardon me, a *what*?"

"An IRG," said Tom. "An Incredibly Revolting Ghost."

And then Hetty Hyssop explained to an astonished Mr. Lovely who had been haunting his house recently, and how she'd found out through Tom.

He stared at the pair of them in disbelief. "Uncle Hugo . . . ?"

". . . fled to the cellar of this young man here. Yes." Hetty Hyssop nodded. "He is the ghost who just gave you such a fright. My friend Tom brought your spooky uncle here in his backpack. He's really quite a harmless kind of ghost, a so-called ASG."

"I'm not that harmless! Didn't you see how he trembled when I scared him? He shook like powdered pudding!" With a grim face Hugo floated out of the backpack again. He inflated himself to full size and wobbled once again toward the horrified Mr. Lovely.

"Your grandfather was right!" he breathed. "I'm Huuugo; I turned into a ghost after a tragic accident more than one hundred fifty years ago. Your late great-great-grandfather was still alive then. So wonderfully easy to scare, he was! Had a lot of respect for me."

"Unbelievable," murmured Mr. Lovely, his knees trembling. "Just unbelievable."

"Mr. Lovely," continued Hetty Hyssop, "we've come to help your great-great-uncle get this house back. Would you be prepared to give Hugo a home if we free you of the IRG?"

"Of course I would!" cried Mr. Lovely. "*He's* never gotten in the way of my cookie-baking. Though he'd jolly well better not scare me again like he just did then."

"Ghosts' honor!" purred Hugo. "I'll just do a little teeny bit of haunting."

"Good, that's all sorted then," said Hetty Hyssop. "Now we must quickly prepare a couple of things." She looked at her watch. "There's less than an hour to go before it gets dark – and then, my dear friends, things will get seriously spooky in here!"

Chattering Teeth and Knocking Knees

"Hmm. Hmm!" Hetty Hyssop looked disapprovingly around Mr. Lovely's drawing room. "Blue – nothing but blue. That isn't good news. And not a mirror in sight."

"Mirror?" asked Mr. Lovely, flummoxed.

Tom set his glasses straight. "Mirrors are very useful against ghosts," he said. "Didn't you know?"

But Mr. Lovely didn't reply. Peculiar things were happening to him. His hair suddenly stood on end, his face went as pale as a mushroom, and his knees started knocking. He was staring at the door with wide-open eyes.

A muffled thumping noise came from the hall. The IRG sensor in Tom's pocket turned as cold as ice.

"It's coming – hide!" cried Hetty Hyssop. Hastily she seized the bucket with the graveyard dirt and disappeared behind an armchair.

Tom didn't wonder what all this meant for long, but dived headlong behind the sofa.

"Oooooooooooh!" moaned Hugo, shrinking into a wobbly ball.

"Get back into the backpack!" cried Tom. "Go on, get in!"

The thumping came closer, accompanied by a hollow howling sound. Mr. Lovely still stood in the middle of the room as if rooted to the spot.

"Get down!" cried Hetty Hyssop from behind the armchair. "Quick – hide!"

"I – I – I – I can't! I can't seem to move!" stammered Mr. Lovely, covering his face with his hands. The thumping reached the door. With a crash it flew open, and a hideous, massive, vile-smelling *something* streamed into the room.

The IRG.

"Baaaaaaaaaaaaaaaaahhhhhh!" it roared, growing as high as the ceiling and making all the lightbulbs explode. Its yellow eyes, pits of bottomless evil, stared down at poor Mr. Lovely. Its gigantic mouth, a good three feet wide, gaped open and let out a foul and violent belch. Then the IRG took a deep breath and

blew its icy breath down onto Mr. Lovely, who froze on the spot.

Tom's teeth chattered like a keyboard. He trembled so much that his glasses slid off his nose. Hugo's horrified wailing could be heard through the backpack. Only Hetty Hyssop kept her nerve. With lightning speed she grabbed a handful of graveyard dirt from the bucket, stood up – and threw it at the IRG's nebulous chest.

"Aaaaaaaaarghhhh!" roared the gigantic ghost, turning as purple as a plum. Its yellow eyes spun around and its icy breath turned as warm as central heating. Bellowing hideously it shot out into the hall. The door slammed shut behind it and a couple of pictures fell off the walls. Then, suddenly, there was a deathly silence.

"Ohboyohboyohboyohboyohboyohboy!" moaned Tom, feeling around for his glasses on the floury carpet.

"We're doomed!" wailed Hugo, wringing his hands as he wobbled out of the backpack. "We're doooomed!"

"Air! We've got to let in some air!" cried Hetty Hyssop. "Or else that IRG stench'll give us all blue spots!" She quickly pushed the curtains aside and yanked the windows open. It was nearly dark outside.

"Aaaaaaahhhhhh!" sighed Hugo. "Ghosting time!"

Oh, not that as well, thought Tom, putting his glasses back on with trembling fingers. Nervously he looked across at Mr. Lovely, who was standing absolutely motionless.

"Frozen through and through!" declared Hetty Hyssop. "We've got to get him to the fireplace – quickly!"

It took all their combined strength to haul the big, fat man over to the fire. Then Hetty Hyssop took a little bottle of red liquid out of her bag and dripped three drops of it onto Mr. Lovely's ice-cold nose. "My special defrosting potion," she explained. "I made it specially to treat people frozen by IRGs." She looked around, shaking her head. "Of course," she muttered. "All the lightbulbs have blown again. Time to light the candles."

Tom sank wearily down into an armchair while Hetty Hyssop positioned her candles.

"Ohboyohboyohboyohboyohboyohboy," he sighed once more. His hands shook. So did his arms. And his legs. In fact, *everything* trembled. He felt like human jelly.

Mr. Lovely, on the other hand, was still standing stock-still by the fire. But his lips were no longer blue, and the tip of his nose was slowly turning pink.

Hetty Hyssop looked at her watch. "Things should be quiet for the moment. A dose of graveyard dirt that size puts most IRGs out of action for at least two hours. That gives us enough time to think about what to do next. I . . ."

She was interrupted by a loud crash. It came from the hall. And it was followed by a gruesome laugh.

"Nooooooo!" howled Hugo and disappeared under the carpet in a flash. Hetty Hyssop and Tom ran to the door and peered out. What they saw was not for the fainthearted.

The whole hall was illuminated by a hideous moldy green light. The IRG, as vast as a hot-air balloon, was floating up by the ceiling, smashing the chandelier.

"Ten minutes!" moaned Hetty Hyssop. "The dirt only worked for ten minutes. That's my whole plan scuppered!"

The IRG took a nosedive to the staircase, slid up the banisters with an earsplitting screech, and raced back down with jet-propelled speed.

"Wooooooooaaaaaaaaargghhhhhhh!" it screeched, juggling a gigantic cupboard and two tables before smashing them against the wall with an excited yell.

"Time for a little test!" whispered Hetty Hyssop, taking an apple out of her coat pocket and letting it roll surreptitiously into the hall. When the IRG spotted the apple, it immediately dropped the chest of drawers it had just been working on and emitted a delighted grunt. Then, quick as lightning, it grabbed the apple and threw it into its wide-open mouth.

"Mmmmmmmmmmmmmm!" it grunted.

"Aha!" Hetty Hyssop whispered in Tom's ear. "It's a Gobble-IRG. This could be our chance!"

The IRG raced back up the stairs. At the top, it took off its head and threw it down the stairs. *Bump-bump-bump,* the head rolled toward the drawing room door, giggling gruesomely. The yellow eyes looked straight at Tom.

"Squint, young friend, squint!" cried Hetty, springing up and kicking the ghost's head back to the staircase like a soccer ball. Then, quick as a flash, she sprang back into the drawing room, grabbed the bucket, and placed herself threateningly in the doorway.

The head rolled toward the stairs, wailing. With a terrible screech, the IRG shot down the stairs, grabbed it with its moldy green fingers, and put it back where it belonged. Then it came floating slowly, ominously slowly, toward the two ghosthunters. Tom trembled so hard that he bit his tongue.

"Baaaaaaaaah!" the IRG groaned. "Yoooooouuuuu waaaaaaiiiiiiit!" Its voice sounded as if it came from the bottom of a well. A very, very deep well.

"You can stop showing off right now!" Hetty Hyssop replied, her voice as calm as if talking to a huge, slimy ghost was the most normal thing in the world. "All this crying and flying and furniture-destroying doesn't impress me in the slightest."

It does me, thought Tom. The stench of the IRG made him dizzy and that wretched squinting gave him a terrible headache. As if that was not enough, he noticed, much to his horror, that his hands were covered in blue spots.

"Goooooo aaaaaawaaaaaay!" bellowed the IRG, growing as high as the ceiling.

"You go away!" Hetty Hyssop retorted. "You go today." And while she spoke, she grabbed some grave-yard dirt in one hand and pulled a perfume atomizer from under her coat with the other.

The IRG shook with sneering laughter and smashed a windowpane. But its yellow eyes flickered, worried, between the bucket and the atomizer.

"The scent of violets," Hetty Hyssop called out to it, "makes ghost skin terribly itchy. And you've already sampled my graveyard dirt."

"Paaaaaah!" grunted the IRG. "Thaaaaat's noth-ing. But weeeeee're in for lots more fun together tooooooonight!"

A hideous smile played around the corners of its ugly mouth and then – *whoosh!* – it vanished. Leaving the hall pitch-black and silent.

"It's gone!" Tom looked around, gobsmacked.

"Yes, but not for long, I fear," said Hetty Hyssop. "This rascal wants to play a bit of cat-and-mouse with us. But I do believe I know how to get rid of him now. Oh yes! Though it's turning into a mighty dangerous business!"

The Plan

They returned to the drawing room on shaky legs. Mr. Lovely had thawed out and was sitting in front of the embers with his nose buried in a handkerchief.

"That's the fifth time it's frozen me!" he sniffed. "I'll end up with pneumonia!"

"You should just thank your lucky stars that nothing worse has happened to you!" Hetty Hyssop put her half-empty bucket and the atomizer on the table and flopped down on the sofa. "If you hadn't kept your eyes shut, it would have exploded you – no two ways about it!"

"Wh-what?" stammered Mr. Lovely, horrified. "Explode? But – but that's terrible! Hideous!"

"It's gone?" Hugo emerged from under the carpet as pale as vanilla. "Have you finally gotten rid of it?"

"Just you keep quiet!" Tom snapped. "Fat lot of help you are. We risk being blown up or deep-frozen for you, and you crawl under the carpet!"

"Psst!" hissed Hetty Hyssop.

A faint scratching came from above their heads. And then suddenly an earsplitting racket broke loose. The radio started blaring; the television sprang to life; and Mr. Lovely's alarm clock began bleeping nonstop.

"Don't panic!" cried Hetty Hyssop amidst all the chaos. "It's just a harmless machinery haunting! IRGs find this highly amusing!"

Exactly at that moment a greenish arm burst through the ceiling directly above her.

"Watch out!" yelled Tom. He grabbed the atomizer, though his hands were still shaking, and sprayed half its contents onto the wobbling fingers.

"Aaaaaarghhh!!" The IRG's screech echoed through

the ceiling, and the spooky hand disappeared into thin air before their very eyes. The radio, the TV, and the alarm clock fell silent.

"Urgh! Violets! On top of everything else!" wailed Hugo, scratching his pale, wobbly body.

Even Hetty Hyssop was somewhat green around her pointy nose. "My dear Tom," she said. "You did amazingly well. Thanks so much."

"Oh, that . . . that was nothing," Tom murmured, but his cheeks burned with pride.

Mr. Lovely sneezed violently. "So what's the plan?" he asked, looking nervously at the ceiling.

"You'll see in a minute," Hetty Hyssop said in a low voice. She took a pen and paper out of her pocket and began to write by the light of a candle. Tom and Mr. Lovely looked over her shoulder, all agog. Even Hugo stopped moaning and floated across. And this is what they read:

Dear friends!

I chose the written word to tell you my plan because the IRG is undoubtedly eavesdropping on us. Read quickly, as we need to destroy this note as soon as possible! As Tom and I discovered in our little experiment, this IRG we're dealing with is a so-called Gobble-IRG, and is very interested in food.

Mr. Lovely started nodding vigorously. "Yes, yes!" he whispered. "It keeps eating all my cookies!"

Hetty Hyssop raised a warning finger to her lips and carried on writing:

As the IRG, astonishingly enough, barely reacts to the external application of graveyard dirt, we have to get it to EAT some. However, I must stress that this has never been done before, as IRGs have a most refined palate. After previous attempts one specimen spat the bait out on the spot and became very, very angry — with serious consequences for its pursuer. Therefore all our hopes rest on you, Mr. Lovely!! You have to invent a cookie that is so irresistible to ghosts that the IRG gobbles it up on the spot. Our friend Hugo will advise you, as he most certainly knows most about ghosts' tastes. You have not *more than an hour. Tom and I will use all the methods at our disposal to keep the IRG away from the kitchen for that long. That, my friends, is my plan. We don't have another chance. Short of running away, that is.*

Hetty Hyssop looked inquiringly at her three coconspirators.

Tom nodded. "OK!" he whispered.

"I'll do my best," whispered Mr. Lovely.

Hugo wobbled around a bit, but then he nodded as well.

"Good!" Hetty Hyssop smiled. "Then I'll destroy the note!" But just as she was holding it into the candle flame, an icy wind blew through the room, tore the note from out of her hand, and extinguished all the candles. Moldy green light radiated from the embers of the fire.

"The note!" cried Hetty Hyssop. "Quick! We have to find it!"

But Tom and Mr. Lovely fumbled around in the darkness in vain. A gruesome moaning came from the fireplace, and the IRG stuck its head out, grinning.

"Hahahahoooohahahahahaha!" it laughed. Its eyes glowed like car headlights.

With all the courage born of despair, Tom rushed toward the monster, his hands filled with graveyard dirt, and sprinkled the wobbling body with the dark dirt.

"Aaaaaaaaargh!" howled the IRG – so loudly that Tom's ears almost dropped off. Hissing like a deflating balloon, the ghost crumpled up, but with its remaining strength it touched Tom's arm. He stumbled and fell. His left arm was as stiff as an icicle. But the IRG disappeared through the wall, still howling.

Hetty Hyssop struck a match. She lit the candles again, looked around her – and flopped onto the sofa, shattered.

"Gone!" she murmured. "That's it. We've lost."

Tom pulled himself together and held out his stiff arm to her. "Could you just drop some of your special thawing-out stuff on this?"

"Of course, my dear!" Hetty Hyssop hastily searched for the little bottle and put a few drops of the bloodred elixir onto his arm. "You really are an extraordinarily brave young man and quite a gifted ghosthunter. But sadly all this bravery won't get us any further. All we can do now is try to escape before this ghost turns us all into ice sculptures." With a sad smile she shook her head. "Nothing like this has ever happened to me in my entire career."

"So do you think," Mr. Lovely sniffled into his handkerchief, "that we have to leave the house? But what about all my baking gear, all my books and cake tins, my sugar decorations, my . . ."

"Leave them," Hetty Hyssop interrupted him. "We have to be out of here before midnight."

"Nonsense!" came a voice from under the sofa. "What a load of nonsense!" And with a smug grin Hugo floated out and let Hetty's handwritten note flutter down onto her lap.

"Oh, that's brilliant!" cried Mr. Lovely. "Quite brilliant!"

But with a warning glance Hetty Hyssop pointed to the ceiling, and then held the note quickly to the candle flame again. This time, luckily, nothing happened, and all that remained of their secret plan was a handful of ashes. Satisfied, Hetty Hyssop brushed them off the table. "Tom? Mr. Lovely? Hugo? Are you all ready?"

The coconspirators nodded.

"Good!" whispered Hetty Hyssop. "Then let's teach this wretched IRG a ghosthunting lesson it will not forget for the rest of its slimy existence!"

The Ghost Hunt

The entrance hall was filled with darkness when Tom and Hetty Hyssop stepped out of the drawing room. A faint clattering could be heard from the kitchen. Mr. Lovely was already at work.

Hetty Hyssop checked her IRG sensor – and smiled.

"We're in luck, Tom," she whispered. "According to the IRG sensor, our friend's upstairs. Which means all we've got to do is make sure he stays up there for another hour. Here –" she pulled two hats out of her unfathomable handbag "– miner's helmets. They've got a little lamp on the front of them. Very practical!"

When Tom put one on, though, it slipped almost down to his nose.

"I'm sorry. I'm afraid they don't come in smaller sizes," whispered Hetty Hyssop. "Are we all ready? Violet perfume? Graveyard dirt? IRG sensor?"

Tom nodded and felt for the last bit of graveyard

dirt in his jean pockets. The rest was with Mr. Lovely in the kitchen, ready to be turned into a portion of irresistible ghost-cookies.

"Good. Then let's go!"

With shaking knees Tom followed the old lady up the big staircase. It was a quarter to nine. The higher up they went, the colder it became. The last few steps were covered with snow.

"A quite common effect of IRG breath," Hetty Hyssop whispered while her boots sank deep into the snow. At the top of the stairs a vast gallery awaited them, stretching around the large hall, with numerous doors, separated from the big drop by nothing but narrow banisters. Tom leaned against them and looked down. The darkness in the hall below was like a black sea.

Hetty Hyssop held out her sensor – and signaled him to follow her. She turned to the left. Side by side they crept over the snowy carpet to the first door. Tom held his IRG sensor tight. It seemed to get colder with every step. Quite an alarming feeling. The door they approached hung off its hinges and the room behind it lay deep in snow. The furniture was stacked up as if a giant child had made a pile of bricks, and a shredded carpet hung from a lamp.

"Good job!" Tom's voice sounded slightly shaky — as shaky as his knees.

Surprisingly the room behind the next door looked almost untouched. No snow, just hoarfrost, no damaged or piled-up furniture . . . and the bed in front of the iced-up window looked as if it hadn't been slept in for at least a hundred years.

"Our slimy friend obviously doesn't like this room," Tom whispered hoarsely.

"Well observed! And there's the reason." Hetty Hyssop pointed at a massive mirrored wardrobe standing behind the door. It didn't have so much as a scratch on it. "Remember this room, Tom," she whispered. "If the IRG chases us, that wardrobe will be a first-rate place to hide."

Tom cleared his throat – and nodded. *"If the IRG chases us . . ."* His knees felt as wobbly as if he had turned into a ghost himself.

Behind the next few doors they found nothing but smashed-up furniture, upside-down pictures, and books covered in slime – and with every step Tom's IRG sensor grew colder. . . .

They had already left the staircase far behind when they suddenly heard something behind the seventh door: the most gruesome piano plunking accompanied by a song that made every single hair on Tom's head stand up and brought tears to his eyes.

I'm coming soooooon
I'm coming soooooon
Aaaaaand . . . I'm gonna scaare the life out of yoooooou!

As quietly as possible they crept closer. Only the snow crunched slightly under their shoes.

"Quite a horrible singer, isn't it?" Hetty Hyssop whispered. "Well, we'll make sure that very soon it won't feel like singing anymore." Then she took a bundle of extralong sparklers out of her bag and planted them in the snow outside the door. Tom watched her in amazement.

"Don't watch me, watch the IRG, young man," Hetty Hyssop muttered. "I'm just taking all necessary precautions."

Obediently Tom peeped through the keyhole. The whole room was bathed in luminous mold green, evaporating from the IRG's huge body. The ghost itself floated above a grand piano, wildly hammering away at the keys with its wobbly fingers. Its head, meanwhile, lay in an armchair, brawling out its hideous song.

"It doesn't look like it's in the mood for departure," Tom reported in a whisper. "It's even taken its head off again!"

"Fine!" Hetty Hyssop whispered back. "Then I'll just have a quick nose around the other rooms while you keep watch here. If the IRG comes out before I get back, light the sparklers right away and spray violet perfume all over it. Only use the graveyard dirt as a last resort! I sha'n't be long!" Then she disappeared into the darkness.

Well, knowing my luck, it'll be out any second now, thought Tom. And at the same moment – the IRG stopped singing. The sudden silence made Tom's heart almost stop as well. His IRG sensor felt so cold that it seemed to be frozen to his skin. Trembling he bent and peeped through the keyhole again. The IRG was still there. It was just chucking its head into the fruit bowl with a great curving throw. But then it suddenly put its head back on and wobbled toward the door.

"Curses!" Tom hastily stepped behind the line of sparklers Hetty Hyssop had planted in the snow. He stuffed his trembling fingers into his jean pocket and pulled out a box of matches. *Fssshhh!* The first sparkler fizzed long white needles of light into the darkness. Quite impressive – obviously a very special kind of ghosthunting sparklers – but Tom's hands shook so hard when he tried to light another that he dropped the box and all the matches fell into the snow. *Nonononono!!!* Desperately he was kneeling down to pick them up . . . when moldy light suddenly colored the snow with ghastly green. The IRG.

Squint, Tom, squint! he thought while he looked up in terror. The IRG was looming above, staring first at him and then at the lone sparkling sparkler. It seemed hypnotized by it. Tom's heart beat like a drum.

What now? The room with the mirrored wardrobe?

Out of reach. The IRG blocked the way. And he
wouldn't be able to light the other sparklers with those
wet matches. *Idiot!* he thought. *Idiotidiotidiot!*

The IRG gulped as if the sparkler's light needles
made it sick. *Maybe I can still run through and get to the
wardrobe?* Tom thought while he was still squinting
down his nose, his mind almost paralyzed with panic.
Didn't people in movies run through ghosts all the time? In
fact the IRG looked slightly transparent . . . and dizzy.
But then the one sparkler went out and the huge ghost

let out a satisfied groan – and grinned. A hideous, limb-trembling, teeth-chattering, heartbeat-stopping grin.

"Hetty!" Tom yelled. And ran. In the direction Hetty Hyssop had taken.

"Help!" he kept yelling. "Help, Hetty Hyssop! It's coooom-iiing!"

The IRG followed him, chuckling wickedly. Tom could feel the icy breath on his neck. *It's going to freeze me,* he thought. *It will. Any second now.*

But all of a sudden Hetty Hyssop rushed toward him. She had a whole bundle of fizzing sparklers in each hand. They surrounded her with white light as if she were sparkling herself!

"Tom, the violet perfume!" she cried. "Quick!"

Puzzled, the IRG paused. It blinked angrily at the sparklers and screwed up its nose, nauseated, as Tom spilled the perfume all over his sweater.

"Baaaaaah! Thaaaaaat woooon't help yooooooou, eeeeeither!" it howled.

"I'm afraid it's right!" Hetty Hyssop breathlessly hissed into Tom's ear. "The sparklers won't last. We'll have to use the rest of the graveyard dirt to get to the mirrored wardrobe. But just use tiny, tiny bits!"

Of course, the graveyard dirt! Tom reached into his pockets, his fingers still wet with snow. "You win, ghost," he heard Hetty Hyssop say. "We give in. Let us pass, and we will leave the house." She grabbed Tom's hand and took a step forward. And another.

"Hooooooohoooooo!" intoned the IRG. "Well thaaaaaat wooooooould suit yoooooou!"

"Tom, the graveyard dirt!" Hetty whispered.

Whizz! Tom threw a pinch of dirt at the IRG's ghostly fingers.

"Oooooow!" it howled, wobbling a step backward.

Whizz! Tom threw another pinch.

Step by step, cursing and howling, the IRG retreated. But they still had two doors to go to reach the room with the mirrored wardrobe, and not a crumb of dirt was left in Tom's pocket.

Hetty Hyssop turned as pale as the ghost. "I'm sorry, Tom!" she whispered hoarsely. "I should never have asked you to come along. What a foolhardy old woman I am! And what a brilliant ghosthunting team we could have been! It's a shame!"

"What kind of ghosts do you think *we* will end up as?" Tom whispered back. "I really hope I won't be an IRG!"

The IRG grinned a malicious grin. "Doooown!" it moaned while its icy fingers pointed over the banisters into the black drop. "I'm going to blow you dooooown there!"

As tightly as he could, Tom grabbed the banisters with one hand and Hetty Hyssop's arm with the other. Then he closed his eyes. He definitely didn't want to die squinting. "Waaaaaaaaaaaahhhhhhhhh!" something howled above him, and cold arms lifted him and Hetty Hyssop above the banisters into thin air.

"Hugo!" cried Tom. "Where did you come from?"

"We've done it!" breathed Hugo. "We've done it!"

Flying just as quickly as an ASG can fly, he made for the kitchen. A delicious smell of cookies wafted out toward them.

"The IRG!" cried Hetty Hyssop. "It's coming!"

It had cost the IRG a moment to get over Hugo's sudden appearance. With a ghastly screech of rage it dived over the banisters and chased after them. In the nick of time Hugo whizzed through the kitchen door. Hastily he lifted Tom and Hetty onto the top of a cupboard and hid beside them.

"Where's Mr. Lovely?" Tom whispered – then

saw two shoes peeping out from behind the long blue curtain that covered the only window.

"Baaaaaarrrrrrgggggghhhhhh!" the IRG came charging in – and stopped abruptly in front of the gigantic baking tray that was standing on the kitchen table. It sniffed, grinned ecstatically – and, with its wobbly fingers, stuffed countless cookies down its cavernous hatch all in one shot.

"One!" whispered Hetty Hyssop.

The IRG belched and rubbed its belly contentedly.

"Two!"

The IRG hiccuped and turned as yellow as a lemon.

"Threeee!" cried Hetty Hyssop.

Ploop! went the IRG, shrinking to the size of a brimstone butterfly. Tom couldn't believe his eyes.

"Hurrah! It worked! The graveyard dirt worked!" cried Hetty Hyssop. She almost fell off the cupboard with excitement. "Quick – catch it, Hugo!"

"My pleasure!" howled Hugo, and whizzed after the IRG. He plucked it out of the air just as it tried to flutter through the door.

"He got it!" cried Mr. Lovely, reappearing from behind the curtain.

"Here, give that to Hugo," cried Hetty Hyssop, throwing him what looked like a perfectly normal jam jar.

"That's safe?" Mr. Lovely said, looking doubtfully at the jar.

"It is indeed," Hetty Hyssop replied, "so would you two please shut the IRG inside it and then get us down!"

"Yooooou meeeeeanie!" shrieked the IRG as Hugo stuffed it into the glass jar. "I'll get my reeeevenge!" However, its terrible voice was nothing but a squeak and it looked quite ridiculous when it flapped its tiny yellow wings against the see-through walls.

"A special glass, guaranteed ghost-proof!" said Hetty Hyssop as Hugo lifted her and Tom down from the cupboard. "My dear Mr. Lovely, your cookies were excellent!"

Mr. Lovely turned as red as one of the cherries he had used as decoration for his cookies. "Uncle Hugo was a great help."

"He was indeed!" Hetty Hyssop said, smiling at Hugo. "I never was so glad to see a ghost as when Tom and I stood up there behind those banisters. Thank you once again, both of you. And I definitely want that cookie recipe. Though luckily IRGs are a very rare ghost species and my chances of meeting another in my ghosthunting career are not that high!"

"It looks hilarious that size," Tom said, grinning into the glass. The IRG angrily threw its head at him. The head was the only part that still looked like its old, evil self – a shrunken version, of course.

"I'll take it home with me first of all," said Hetty Hyssop. "And tomorrow we'll all get together for a nice cup of tea to celebrate our victory – of course with some of Mr. Lovely's cookies, too. If possible a variety without graveyard dirt!"

"Home? Oh no!" cried Tom, looking at the time. "I'd better get to Grandma's before she sounds the alarm."

"I'll fly yoooou there," breathed Hugo. "As a fare-well gift!"

"Oh, don't think you'll get rid of me that easily! I'll come and visit you," said Tom. "If Mr. Lovely doesn't mind!"

"On the contrary!" said Mr. Lovely. "I'll bake you a very special cake each time you come. I am indebted to you for the rest of my life, young man, and I guess I can say the same for Hugo!"

"Oh, it . . . it was nothing!" Tom replied, fumbling with his glasses. "However, Hugo, you could actually do me a massive favor. . . ."

"Oh? What?" asked Hugo curiously.

"Well, you know I've got a big sister," said Tom. "A sister who doesn't believe in ghosts. Do you think you could convince her she's wrong?"

"Ooooh, I'd love to!" said Hugo, smiling delightedly. "Right away?"

Tom shook his head, yawning. "No, Friday would be best. As soon as it's dark. Just knock on my window."

"Absoluuuutely, absoluuuutely!" Hugo rubbed his icy hands in anticipation. "Is your sister very easily scared?"

"Oh no," said Tom. "But you'll find a way."

Revenge

Friday was the day that Mom and Dad went out.
Pretty much every Friday evening they left Tom to
be looked after by his deeply caring big sister. Lola, of
course, would have preferred to meet up with her
eternally giggling friends — and took it out on Tom.

This Friday was no exception.

They'd barely been alone five minutes when Lola
sat down with the phone glued to her ear to tell all
her friends what a nightmare it was looking after her
stupid, silly squirt of a thickhead brother, just because
he'd wet himself with fear if he were left on his own.

Next she announced: "I'm afraid the film isn't
suitable for 'children under twelve,' little brother," and
switched off the TV right in front of Tom's nose. Then
she resorted to violence to confiscate the chocolate that
Grandma had given Tom, supervised his toothbrushing
with an egg timer — and then gave him her generous

permission to read in bed for an hour. Just like every Friday.

But this time Tom didn't lie there grinding his teeth while the TV blared away in the next room. This time he waited for Hugo.

His ghostly friend appeared as silently as moonlight when darkness was already filling Tom's room like black soup. Hugo just floated through the wall.

"Helloooo!" he breathed. "I'm here. As promised."

"She's in the living room!" whispered Tom, standing up. "Come on, I'll take you there."

Silently he opened the bedroom door and crept out into the hall. Hugo floated behind him, humming softly.

The living room door was open a crack. Lola always did that to make sure Tom could hear her laughing at the TV.

"Right," whispered Tom. "Just as you promised, OK?"

"Ooooh yes!" moaned Hugo gleefully. Then he disappeared through the door. Tom turned and shot back into his bedroom. He switched on the light and threw himself on his bed.

Next door the TV suddenly went silent. Instead there was a shrill, small scream – and next minute Lola

came rushing into Tom's room, pale and trembling. She quickly locked the door and leaned against it.

"Wow, that must be some exciting film," said Tom, setting his glasses straight. "I thought there were only some boring reruns on."

Lola gasped for breath. "There's a gh – a . . . a ghost sitting on the sofa!" she blurted out with a croak.

"Oh, one of those ghosts that don't exist?" asked Tom nonchalantly. "Tell it I said hello."

"Cut out the stupid jokes!" snapped Lola. "It's an enormous creature! It, it – it's eating all the chocolate and moaning and rolling its eyes!"

"Hmm, well," said Tom, his eyes still glued to the pages of his book. "Ghosts don't have particularly good manners. But when all's said and done, you eat my chocolate, too. I think there's still a bar left in the kitchen cupboard, by the way."

"What – what in the world are you saying?" panted Lola. "It's a *ghost*! Don't you get it, you lame-brain? A real ghost! It made the lightbulbs explode and covered everything in slime. We've got to call the police!"

"Ha-ha. So are they supposed to handcuff it or what?" Tom giggled.

"There's nothing to giggle about, you idiot!" screeched Lola.

Tom snapped his book shut with a sigh. "So how big is it exactly?"

"Enormous!" wailed Lola. "It's wobbling right up to the ceiling."

"Aw, then it's just a pretty small specimen," said Tom. "Unlock the door again. I'll just have a look at it."

"Whaaat? Have you gone nuts?"

"*You're* nuts if you think ghosts are put off by locked doors. They just float through them."

Horrified, Lola backed away from the door.

Tom smiled sympathetically as he pushed past her. Confidently he went into the dark living room. Hugo, flickering a kind of blue-green, floated above Lola's armchair, sucking on a bar of chocolate.

"Do you see it?" Lola peeped over Tom's shoulder, her teeth chattering slightly. "Isn't – isn't it hor-hor-horrible?"

"Whatever. It's an Averagely Spooky Ghost. Nothing to worry about."

"What? What are you talking about?"

"Pssst!" Tom cleared his throat. "Hey, ghost," he said loudly. "Get lost, do you hear? And kindly let my sister watch TV in peace."

"Waaaaaaaaaaaah!" howled Hugo, inflating himself threateningly and stretching his icy fingers out toward Tom. He was really outdoing himself.

Lola disappeared into her room, screaming.

"Perfect!" whispered Tom. Then he called loudly enough for Lola to hear: "You don't have to show off! You might be able to scare my sister, but not me. Get lost, or I'll knock your haunting powers out of you forever!"

"Aaaaaaaaooooooohhhh!" moaned Hugo, giving Tom a conspiratorial grin. "Oooooowoooooohooooo!"

"Right!" cried Tom. "This is your last warning. Remember: Violets! Graveyards! Mirrors!"

"Ooooooohhooo!" howled Hugo, pretending to be horrified.

"Get lost!" Tom cried again. "Now!"

With a heartrending sigh — and a friendly wave — Hugo floated toward the window.

"See yooooou later, my friend!" he breathed. Then he disappeared outside into the night.

All was quiet in the living room.

The TV flickered silently away to itself.

Tom walked over to Lola's room and knocked at the door. Tentatively she stuck out the tip of her nose.

"You can come out again," said Tom. "It's gone."

Lola took a step forward and peeped disbelievingly into the living room. Then she looked at her little brother, dumbstruck. "You — you actually got rid of it."

Tom shrugged. "Wasn't difficult. Good night."

The TV stopped flickering and some police cars appeared on the screen, chasing what looked like an alien.

"Don't you want to come and watch with me for a bit?" asked Lola. She peered anxiously behind the sofa. "It's a great movie, and I won't tell Mom!"

"No, thanks," said Tom and yawned. "I know this one. Actually it's dead boring. . . ."

Then he went into his bedroom. He sat on the windowsill with a deep sigh and looked up at the moon.

This is the best night of my whole life, he thought. *The best by miles.*

Lola never called Tom a stupid, silly squirt of a thickhead brother again. In fact Friday evenings became positively cozy, as Lola suddenly developed a marked dislike of watching TV on her own. And she never stole Tom's chocolate again. In short she became a tolerable big sister.

But what became of the other heroes of this story?

Well, Hetty Hyssop delivered several highly regarded lectures on driving out particularly dangerous IRGs and was often invited to tea by Mr. Lovely. He sold his cookie recipe – leaving out the bit about grave-yard dirt, of course – under the name "Ghostly Kisses" to a big cookie factory, and it became a very famous brand.

Hugo cheerfully and contentedly continued haunting the old villa.

And as for the IRG – well, it's still in the jar on

a shelf at the RCFCAG – the Retention Center for Criminally Aggressive Ghosts. At first it wobbled around angrily – but recently you might think it was starting to grow again. . . .

In Case of
an Encounter

Honorable readers, now that you've read of the dangers Tom faced in *Ghosthunters and the Incredibly Revolting Ghost!*, it is most expressly urged that you not be so imprudent as to undertake a similarly perilous expedition. But for those beginning ghosthunters who, all advice to the contrary, insist upon attempting to expel a ghost . . . some words of caution:

PRECAUTIONARY MEASURES
against Ghosts in General

• The color red – as in socks, sweaters, curtains, sofas, and so on.

• Raw eggs, for throwing.

• Violet-scented perfume: ASGs and IRGs alike detest the smell. It makes their skin itch, and it has the added bonus of combating their natural and naturally

foul ghost odor. For best results, spritz via an
atomizer.

- Mirrors: Hang them on your red-painted walls; wear
pocket-sized varieties when in the field.

- A spare pair of shoes: Depending on the variety of
ghost, it will leave a trail that's sticky, snowy, etc. If
in the thrill of the chase your sneakers get glued in
place, it helps to have a backup.

- Graveyard dirt that's been gathered at night (*see
specifics per species below*).

- And no matter what, do not – do NOT – carry a
flashlight on ghosthunting expeditions. The beam of
a flashlight will drive a ghost into a violent rage.

IN CASE OF AN ENCOUNTER WITH AN ASG
(Averagely Spooky Ghost)

- Outfit yourself with a hot water bottle. ASGs
abhor heat.

- Broadcast music at full volume: Mozart is recommended, though in an emergency Beethoven or any of the lesser German composers will suffice.

- Expose it to daylight.

- Douse it with graveyard dirt: An ASG will turn to dust on contact.

IN CASE OF AN ENCOUNTER WITH AN IRG
(Incredibly Revolting Ghost)

- Confront it between the hours of seven and eight p.m., when it is at its weakest.

- Keep it at bay with sparklers (*note: as sparklers only sparkle for so long, this should not be your primary means of defense*).

- Trick it into eating graveyard dirt (*note: this is easier said than done*).

- Worst-case scenario, hide behind the nearest available mirrored wardrobe.

Indispensable Alphabetical
APPENDIX OF ASSORTED GHOSTS

ASG	**A**veragely **S**pooky **G**host
BLAGDO	**BLA**ck **G**host **DO**gs
BOSG	**BO**g and **S**wamp **G**host
CG	**C**ellar **G**host
COHAG	**CO**mpletely **HA**rmless **G**host
FG	**F**ire **G**host
FOFIFO	**FO**ggy **FI**gure **FO**rmer
FOFUG	**FO**ggy **FU**g-**G**host
GG	**G**raveyard **G**host
GHADAP	**GH**ost with **A DA**rk **P**ast
GIHUFO	**G**host **I**n **HU**man **FO**rm
GILIG	**G**ruesome **I**nvincible **LI**ghtning **G**host
HIGA	**HI**storical **G**hostly **A**pparition
IRG	**I**ncredibly **R**evolting **G**host
MUWAG	**MU**ddy **WA**ters **G**host
NEPGA	**NE**gative **P**rojection of a **G**hostly **A**pparition

PAWOG	**PA**le **WO**bbly **G**host
STKNDG	**ST**inking **KNO**cking **G**host
TIBIG	**TI**ny **BI**ting **G**host
TOHAG	**TO**tally **HA**rmless **G**host
TOMOB	**TO**tally **MO**ldy **B**aroness
WHIWHI	**WHI**rlwind **WHI**rler

Miscellaneous Listing of
NECESSITOUS EQUIPMENT AND
NOTEWORTHY ORGANIZATIONS

CDEGH	**C**linic for the **DE**-spookification of **G**host**H**unters
CECOCOG	**CE**ntral **CO**mmission for **CO**mbating **G**hosts
COCOT	**CO**ntact-**CO**mpression **T**rap
FIGHD	**FI**fth **G**host**H**unting **D**iploma
GES	**G**hostly **E**nergy **S**ensor
GHOSID	**GHO**st-**SI**mulation **D**isguise
LOAG	**L**ist **O**f **A**ll Known **G**hosts
NENEB	**NE**gative-**NE**utralizer **B**elt
OFFCOCAG	**OFF**ice for **CO**mbating **CA**stle **G**hosts
RCFCAG	**R**etention **C**enter **F**or **C**riminally **A**ggressive **G**hosts
RICOG	**R**esearch **I**nstitute for **CO**mbating **G**hosts
ROGA	**R**egister **O**ffice for **G**hostly **A**pparitions
SGHD	**S**econd **G**host**H**unting **D**iploma
THGHD	**TH**ird **G**host**H**unting **D**iploma

Coming Soon!

GhosthunterS and the

Gruesome Invincible Lightning GhOst!

The next book
in the ghastly fantastic

GhosthunterS

S E R I E S

*Turn the page for a goose-bump-producing,
shiver-inducing sneak peek . . .*

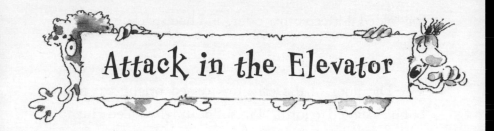

Attack in the Elevator

"I suggest we only go as far as the third floor!" said Hetty Hyssop when the elevator door closed behind them. "And then we'll creep up the stairs. OK?"

Tom nodded, and pressed the button.

"Can I fiiiiinally come out?" grumbled Hugo, wobbling out of the backpack. He looked around, astonished. "What's all this?" With a jolt the elevator started moving, and Hugo was jerked against the wall.

"Help!" he wailed. "Help! What's going on?"

Tom giggled. "It's an elevator, you dumbo!"

"Oh, really?" Irritated, Hugo blew his moldy breath into Tom's face. "And what use is that to anyone?"

"Ssh! Just be quiet!" Hetty Hyssop looked anxiously at her feet. "Do you notice anything?"

Tom looked down. He could feel something warm, very warm, beneath the soles of his shoes. Fortunately his shoes, like Hetty Hyssop's, were filled with aluminum foil folded thirteen times over, and had specially coated soles.

"What's that?" he whispered.

The floor of the elevator turned bright red and bubbles started to form. "I'm suffocating!" wailed Hugo, and floated up to the ceiling.

But it was no cooler there, either.

"Watch out!" cried Hetty Hyssop, and she and Tom clung to each other. The elevator went faster and faster, as if someone were shoving it along from below.

Any second now we'll go through the roof, thought Tom. He squeezed his eyes tightly shut, but that made it even worse. So he opened them again – only to see a fiery finger boring a hole through the red-hot floor. Tom jumped back with a yell.

Another finger appeared, and another, and another, until an entire hand was poking up through the floor, fiery red and steaming. *Snap!* It made a grab for Tom's legs.

Hugo was hanging beneath the ceiling, howling like a dog. Hetty Hyssop, however, sprang protectively in front of Tom, who was trembling and kicking wildly, and threw sugar lumps all over the fiery hand.

Like frightened worms, the fingers jerked back and disappeared into the floor, hissing as they went.

The elevator raced on, braked sharply, plunged back down, whistling as it went, and rattled up again. The ghosthunters desperately tried to stay on their feet. Tom kept bashing the emergency brake, but nothing happened. Then with a terrible jolt that almost threw them flat onto the red-hot floor, the elevator finally stopped. Groaning, it hung on its cables.

"What – what's wrong now?" whispered Tom. He got the answer at once.

With a hiss the elevator door opened and a truly repulsive fiery red head with eyes like lightbulbs grinned at them. It opened its massive mouth, and yellow ghostly flames licked Tom's legs.

"The icing!" cried Hetty. "Go on, Tom!"

His fingers trembling, Tom shot the rest of the icing into the fiery mouth.

The grisly creature clearly didn't like the taste. It had a terrible attack of hiccups that shook the elevator as if it were a baby's rattle. Hetty Hyssop grabbed the baking tray from her back and banged it hard on the gruesome ghost's head. With a belch the head disappeared into thin air.

The door banged shut and the elevator hung clanking and groaning in the air somewhere between the floors.

"It's turning cooler again!" whispered Tom. He was still trembling slightly. His icing baster was empty; Hetty Hyssop's baking tray lay on the ground, dented beyond repair.

"That certainly wasn't any normal Fire Ghost!" grumbled Hugo, floating gently to the ground.

"No, it certainly wasn't!" Hetty Hyssop tried to fix her baking tray onto her back again. She looked very irritated. "That Bigshot played down the problem so much that we almost ended up as incense sticks. He's in for it — *if* we ever get out of here in one piece!" The tip of her nose was positively hot with rage. "What do you think, Tom? Should we go up or down?"

"Up," he replied.

"Up? What do yooou mean, up?" Hugo waggled his icy fingers around indignantly under Tom's nose. "Doesn't anyone care what I think?"

"Nah," said Tom. "In any case, you run off and hide the moment things get a bit tricky!"

"Fine. *Fine.* If that's how yooou want things!" Hugo folded his white arms across his chest. "Then yooou can save yooourselves from this thing. I'm not helping yooou! No: I have my pride, toooo!" And with that he disappeared into Tom's backpack.

"Pass me the sparc baster," demanded Tom.

Hugo's white hand emerged and threw the baster at Tom's head. Tom just grinned and pressed the button for the third floor once more. The elevator set off again with a jolt, and rattled as it flew upward.

"My dear Tom," said Hetty Hyssop. "You really are a remarkably brave young man. I simply couldn't have a better assistant!"

"Oh, it's nothing!" murmured Tom, straightening his glasses in embarrassment.

Then the elevator stopped.

But not on the third floor.

It stopped on the fourth.